SUNSET ON WHISLING ISLAND

A WHISLING ISLAND NOVEL

JULIA CLEMENS

PICKLED PLUM PUBLISHING

*For my Grandma Clemens
You saw this before I did.*

ONE

BESS TOOK a step back and looked at the man she'd woken up next to, stood with, and cared for every day for the last thirty years; it was almost as if she was seeing him for the first time.

They were supposed to be celebrating thirty years of wedded bliss next month. She thought she knew him inside and out. Her entire life had revolved around him and their children. Those were just some of the reasons why she couldn't wrap her mind around what he'd just said.

"Bessie, please. Stop staring at me like that and say something," Jon pleaded with her. But honestly, Bess had no idea what to say to this man who suddenly felt like a stranger. Other than that she hated the way he'd said her name. What had once felt like an adorable term of endearment—Jon was the only one to ever call her Bessie—now made her feel like an old cow.

"Don't call me that," Bess said, knowing that Jon calling her Bessie was a minor offense, especially after the bombshell he'd just dropped on her. But with the way Jon's revelation was bouncing around in her mind like the ball in a pinball machine, taking her to the brink of crushing her soul, Bess had to start somewhere small. Bessie being the worst pet name known to mankind seemed like a good place to start.

"Don't call you Bessie?" Jon's eyes went wide in confusion, and Bess couldn't blame him. Of all the things for her to call him out on, this was probably low on the priority list. Besides, he'd been calling her Bessie since before their wedding day.

"Yes," Bess said, taking a quick glance at the man standing on the other side of the kitchen they'd practically built together.

When they'd bought this fixer upper fifteen years ago, she and Jon had known nothing about remodeling—other than that Bess had an affinity for any television show that did a big home reveal at the end. But when they'd toured properties all over Whisling Island, none of them had boasted a view of the cove like this one. And Bess had to have it. So the two of them had spent a lot of time watching internet tutorials and trading favors with friends who actually knew what they were doing. Three years of toil and strife later, the home had become Bess' dream.

But as she looked at the blue and white striped wallpaper that was now beginning to peel at the edges, she felt a little like that kitchen—once the fulfillment of all her aspirations but now needing some TLC. However, what Jon had just told her would take more than a bit of TLC to get over. Could they ever recover from this? Did Bess even want to?

She knew her trust in Jon was shattered. The man had held her heart so tenderly for years. Shouldn't she have seen the signs, noticed any warnings? Now she felt stupid on top of being blindsided. What kind of woman didn't know that her husband was cheating on her?

"Bess," Jon pleaded again as he crossed the dark wood floors that Bess had painstakingly laid and then proceeded to clean every day since.

Jon dropped to his knees in front of where Bess sat at their gorgeous kitchen table. She had taken months to find just the right one. The color matched perfectly with the wood floors, and when the extra leaf inserts were put in, it was big enough to seat twelve people comfortably.

Bess had wanted to entertain. She'd wanted her home to be the place where her kids and their friends, extended family, and Jon's colleagues wanted to congregate. And it had been. She'd had more dinners and parties than she could remember, many of them right at this very table.

Because the table and floors were so dark, Bess had painted all of the cabinets white and brought in a white quartz countertop that brightened up the room. The kitchen window that sat just above the enormous sink, one of Bess' favorite parts of the kitchen, let in tons of light and a view of her lush, green front yard along with the other homes on Bess' little cove. It was a perfect balance of light and dark, modern and rustic.

"What are you thinking, Bess?" Jon asked, still on his knees so that he was eye to eye with her as she sat.

What was she thinking? Not what she should be thinking about. Shouldn't she ask Jon why? But Bess didn't want to know the why or the how or the when or any of it. Honestly, she didn't want to talk to Jon about anything.

"Bess, I can't lose you," Jon said as he leaned forward in an attempt to take Bess' hands, but that wasn't going to happen. She didn't want this man to touch her.

Bess pushed back in her seat so that she was out of Jon's reach, and it was easy to read the pain on his face. Even if she hadn't studied this same face for the last thirty years, that would have been plain to see.

But he didn't get to be hurt. She shouldn't have to care. Should she? This was brand new ground. Ground she'd never assumed she'd have to cover. So now what?

Bess looked at her watch and realized that if she didn't leave soon, she was going to be late. And Bess hated to be late. She'd always lived by the motto that if she cared about the person she was meeting, she had to be punctual to show them that their time was important to her. And the gathering she was attending was going to be full of people she appreciated and cared about. So she was going to be on time.

She stood and Jon looked up, startled at her sudden movement.

"Don't say anything to the kids," Bess said, and Jon nodded, hope filling his eyes.

She assumed he was hopeful because he thought if she wasn't going to say anything to their children, she wanted to work things out with him. Because, apparently, even though he had broken her trust in the worst kind of way, Jon still wanted her. Needed her, according to him. But then how could he have done this to her? She didn't understand it. She needed to process it. And that was the only reason she didn't want her kids to know anything.

"I have to go," Bess said, unwilling to explain any of what she was thinking to Jon. He didn't deserve her thoughts. He didn't deserve her.

"Go?" Jon asked, and like usual, it was clear her husband had forgotten that she had plans that evening. She had his schedule memorized a month in advance, but heaven forbid he take more than a passing glance at the life she was living.

"The reunion," Bess said, feeling more hurt than she typically would've that Jon had, once again, forgotten something that was important to her. But wasn't this the way it'd always been?

"Right, right. I'm sorry. I forgot." Jon gave the flippant apology he usually did. But *was* he sorry?

Bess narrowed her eyes as she took in everything about her husband. His thick brown hair that was beginning to cover less of his forehead; his black, wire-rimmed, square-framed glasses that showcased brown eyes which had once upon a time made Bess melt with just one look; his long, slim nose; and his small mouth. Bess had used to marvel that such a small mouth could fill the room with so many truths; she'd admired Jon's wisdom and wit for as long as she'd known him. He had always stood up so straight and proud. His shoulders may not have been as broad and wide as some other men, but Jon carried himself in a way that had women taking a second glance. He wore his favorite navy sweater tucked into a pair of Dockers, his typical uniform as a professor of British literature at the small private university that was just a ferry ride away from Whisling Island.

She went back to his eyes and tried to look deep. Did she see sorrow in them? Maybe. She just didn't know anymore. And honestly, she was sick of looking at Jon.

Bess sidestepped her husband and then walked through the kitchen to the garage, not seeing or feeling anything as she did so. Why was she feeling nothing? Shouldn't she be angry or hurt or something? Instead it felt like she was seeing her entire life through a hazy filter, one that kept her from really experiencing anything.

She opened the door of her practical four-door, gray sedan. She'd had a minivan for the years that she'd raised her children, but when her baby, James, had moved into the dorms at the University of Washington three years before, Jon had surprised her with the smaller car she'd always wanted. Parking spaces on the island were always tiny, and Bess hated navigating them with her large minivan.

As Bess sat in the front seat and opened the garage door, she realized she was tired. Every limb felt as though it was too heavy to lift, and as she placed her hands on the steering wheel, she felt the inexplicable urge to close her eyes. But she couldn't give in to that feeling. She needed to go to this reunion tonight.

She'd been thrilled when she'd received the invitation from

Whisling High's class of 1999. Bess had gone back to work for that one year after her youngest's first birthday. She had missed being a teacher in the classroom, her job before she'd been blessed with her little ones, and with a five-, three-, and one-year-old at home, she'd been overwhelmed with the job of mother. So after many, many hours of discussion, she and Jon had decided she should go back to teaching English at the high school.

It had taken just a few weeks of working for Bess to miss her kids like crazy and want to be back home with them full-time, but she'd stuck it out for her students that year. And now, twenty years later, getting an invitation from the class telling her they wanted her to be one of the few faculty members they invited to their reunion had been a beautiful surprise. That one year she'd spent out of the home had made a difference.

Bess turned off of her street and onto Elliot Drive which, considering its mundane name, shouldn't have afforded the views it did. Elliot Drive took her right past the edge of her cove and along the rest of the beautiful beaches and dark blue water that Whisling Island had to offer. The Drive, as many on the island called it, circled the entire island and never left one wanting.

Bess had lived on Whisling Island all her life, only leaving to go to college in Oregon where she'd met Jon. After he'd experienced just one trip back to Whisling with Bess, she knew Jon had fallen in love with her hometown, and it was only a matter of time before he fell in love with her.

Or at least she thought he had. Could a man in love do what Jon had done? Had he ever loved her? The questions came at her hard and fast, and Bess had to sweep them away or risk getting into an accident. She had no answers for them anyway.

The two-lane Drive took her toward town, the hub of most of the activity on the island. It was where many of the bed and breakfasts, which were always full of tourists, were located, along with the quaint town hall and more than a dozen restaurants, most of them boasting the delicious seafood Whisling was known for.

The reunion was going to be held at one of those restaurants since there were only 84 Whisling High graduates in 1999. In fact, the school had never had a graduating class of more than 100 students. And thank goodness because the island didn't have many places that could accommodate a crowd larger than that.

Bess slid her compact car into one of the open spaces just in front of Seascape Restaurant and just off the Drive. There was a larger parking area on the other side of the street, but Bess had seen the closer, open spot and taken it. At least one thing had gone right for her that evening.

Before taking off her seatbelt, she just sat. She watched as couples and small groups of tourists walked up and down both sides of the Drive. Bess' car sat facing the ocean side, but the restaurant was blocking most of her view. Even though the Drive was a main thoroughfare around the island, traffic always slowed down in the middle of town where people were endlessly parking on the sides of the road or even stopping to let off a passenger or two.

What was she doing here? The reunion committee would have understood if Bess had canceled. Could she get out of her car and face so many other humans while her entire life as she knew it was falling apart? Granted, it didn't feel like it was falling apart. Her brain knew what Jon had told her was life altering, but her body didn't seem to be catching up. It was just so tired. Bess leaned her head on the steering wheel, debating whether she should just pull out of her spot and drive home. But then what would she do? Jon was there, and he'd want to talk to her. That was the last thing she wanted. She didn't want to see or hear from Jon for a long time.

With that thought, Bess pulled out her phone and began a text message.

Please be out of the house before I come home tonight.

She read her message before she sent it and decided it wasn't quite right. She adjusted it and then sent, *Be out of the house before I come home tonight.*

The response was immediate.

Please, Bess. Just talk to me. I know what I did was unforgiveable, but we have to talk.

Bess felt the stirrings of anger in her chest and felt relieved that she was feeling something.

We don't have to do anything. And if what you did was unforgiveable, why are you asking me to forgive you? I have nothing to say right now, Jon. I will let you know when I do. Be out of the house.

Bess had never spoken to her husband in such a manner. She'd never spoken to anyone like that. She believed that kindness was usually the best policy, but in this case, her policy was going out the window. Why should she walk around on eggshells trying to keep from hurting Jon when he hadn't considered her at all?

Bess turned off her phone and stuck it into her purse. That's where it would stay all night.

A knock sounded at her window, causing Bess to jump, and she looked up to see her sister, Gen, smiling and facing her with her hands in the air—the universal sign for *what the heck are you doing?*

Bess opened her car door, letting in the chilly January air. She pulled her coat tighter around her as she stepped out of the car and closed her door behind her.

"No Jon tonight?" Gen asked.

Bess shook her head. Would Jon be by her side at anything ever again? Bess had no idea.

"Busy with work?" Gen asked.

Bess nodded, hating that she was lying to her sister but not ready to tell anyone the truth.

Gen, although Bess' sister, was fifteen years her junior. Bess still remembered the joy she'd felt when her mother had announced that Bess was finally going to have a sibling. She knew that her parents had been trying for years and had all but given up hope. Bess had begged for a baby sister until she was old enough to realize that there was nothing more her parents could do and that she was only hurting them with her heartfelt requests. But then Gen came along, a light to all who got to meet her.

"Are you ready for your twenty-year reunion?" Bess asked her sister as they linked arms and headed into the restaurant. She pasted on a smile that even her sister would think was genuine and promised herself to forget about Jon and what he'd done for the rest of the evening. Bess had been looking forward to tonight for months now. She wasn't going to let it be tainted.

"No. When did I get so old?" Gen moaned, and Bess laughed. If Gen was old, Bess wasn't sure what that made her.

"Thankfully you still look hot, even in your golden years." Levi, Gen's husband, joined them just as they walked past the hostess and into the main room that the reunion committee had rented out for the evening.

Gen swatted at her husband playfully, and Bess let go of her sister so that she could walk into her reunion with Levi. Levi, like Jon, was a transplant who had grown to not only love the island but also its laidback lifestyle. If anyone was suited for Whisling life, it was Levi.

"Gen! Mrs. Wilder!" Evelyn, a member of the reunion

committee, called out from a table she'd set up just beyond the hostess station. She stood and gave Gen a hug.

Bess bristled at the mention of her name and wasn't sure why. The name had been hers for thirty years, but hearing it out loud after Jon's revelation reminded her that the name had once been just his. Did the fact that it already didn't feel like hers mean that her subconscious was already seeking a divorce? Is that what she wanted?

"Bess," Gen hissed, and Bess realized Evelyn must have said more that Bess had missed.

"Excuse me, I'm not sure where my head is today. But please, call me Bess since we're all adults now," Bess said with a smile that felt a little forced. She noticed Gen's second look at her face, and Bess realized she needed to hide her feelings better if she wanted her secret to stay that way.

"Perfect," Eveline said as she took a couple of nametags from the pile next to her and then a permanent marker. "Bess," she said as she wrote the first tag, followed by Gen's nametag.

Eveline looked up at Levi, and Gen grinned as she said, "This is my plus one and husband, Levi."

"Of course. Your pictures on social media don't do either of you justice. You are one lucky guy, Levi," Eveline said as she wrote Levi's name on the final tag. "Gen has always been quite the catch."

"Oh, please. If anyone's the catch here, it's you. I'm not the one who got swept off her feet and now lives in a New York penthouse apartment," Gen said with a grin at Eveline.

"Did you get all of that from my social media posts?" Eveline asked, her cheeks turning a little red as if she hadn't meant to boast about her life.

"No. That was all gossip from my salon," Gen said with a wink.

Eveline laughed. "That's right. You're a world-class hair dresser now," Eveline said.

Gen guffawed. "Not quite world-class," Gen said with a shake of her head, but Levi stepped forward and put an arm around Gen's shoulders as he said, "She definitely is."

It was now Gen's turn to blush, but since the restaurant door had opened to let in a new group, it was time to move on.

"Great to see you, Eveline. How long are you in town?" Gen asked as she stepped aside to let the next group forward.

"Until next week. We extended our normal holiday visit for the reunion," Eveline said, and Gen nodded.

Bess knew that was one of the reasons they'd held this reunion in early January. Nearly half of the graduating class had left the island for college and had never come back. But most of them would come home for at least the holidays, so it was the best time to catch most of them.

"We'll have to do lunch sometime before you go," Gen said.

"Definitely. Text me," Eveline said before turning her attention to the next group.

Bess turned her attention from Eveline and the sign-in table to the rest of the room. The round tables were covered with white tablecloths. In the center of each of them was a gold '99 surrounded by white sea shells and blue sea stones, the color scheme perfect for Whisling High's colors of blue and gold.

The other decorations in the room were minimal. A few blue and gold balloons were tied to the buffet table, and there was an enormous blue and gold balloon archway that stood next to the wall behind Eveline. Bess was going to guess that was a place for photo opportunities. The main focus of the room that night and every night at the Seascape Restaurant was the view of the ocean. This side of the Drive had very little beach, so when Bess looked out the window, it almost felt like she was on the glassy, blue water.

Bess looked around the room and found one other non-nine-tyniner, another teacher. But since she'd only taught for that one year, she and Mrs. Neely were acquaintances at best.

The island was relatively small, but that didn't mean everyone who lived there was friends. The sheer number of tourists who came to the island doubled and sometimes tripled the local population, so the extra people made the island seem a lot less intimate. There were even other lifers, like Bess, who Bess had never met.

Bess considered joining Mrs. Neely at her table, though, since she wasn't sure where else to go. Teachers should stay with teachers, right?

"Where are you going?" Gen asked as Bess took a few steps toward the table where Mrs. Neely sat.

"To the teachers' table," Bess said as she pointed to Mrs. Neely.

"Hate to break it to you, Bess, but there will be no teachers' table. You and Neely were the only ones invited. I guess many of my classmates don't have fond memories of the rest of you all. Although I loved all of my teachers," Gen said with a smirk that Levi laughed at. Gen had been known to be a bit of a brown noser in high school, and Levi had heard enough stories to know of Gen's reputation.

"Sit with us," Gen offered, but Bess knew that wouldn't be fair to her sister. This was supposed to be her night to reunite with her past friends. Besides, Bess wanted to spend the evening in the periphery, which wouldn't be possible if she was with Gen. Gen had always been quite popular.

"I think I'll go see if Eveline has anything I can help with," Bess said.

Gen shook her head, knowing exactly what her sister was doing. "It'll be more fun if you hang out with us," Gen said.

Bess smiled. "For me or for you?" she asked.

"For both of us," Gen said.

Bess smiled again as she shook her head. She couldn't accept Gen's invitation, but despite that, she was so grateful for her sister. Little did Gen know what she was doing for Bess' flagging spirit.

"I'll join you later," Bess said.

Gen shrugged. "I can't assure there will still be space at our table. You know how popular I am." She laughed as if it was all a joke, but Bess and Levi knew the truth. Gen was like a flame that everyone wanted to come near to bask in her warmth. Too bad it was much harder for her sister to see that about herself.

"I'll take my chances," Bess said as she walked over to where Eveline sat greeting another couple. Bess glanced around the room and noticed most everyone in the room had come in pairs. Mrs. Neely was also on her own—she'd lost her husband a few years before, so Bess was glad to see that her table was beginning to fill with some of her old students who seemed thrilled to spend the night with their favorite teacher from high school.

Bess felt a little bit like a chaperone at a dance. Maybe she shouldn't have come. She could have kicked Jon out and ... then what? Spent the night reliving everything that could have been the reason things had gone so wrong? No. It was better that she was here, and she knew she'd feel much more like herself after she was given a job.

"Mrs. Wilder," Benson, one of her favorite students, said as he nearly ran across the room to give her a hug.

"Benson," Bess said happily, returning his hug.

Benson had been a young man who she was sure would have a promising future, and he'd lived up to her expectations and more. He'd been one of the many to leave the island after high school, but, thanks to gossip central (i.e. Gen's salon), Bess was kept up-to-date with most of the happenings on and off the island. According to Benson's mother, he was working as a law clerk to one of the Supreme Court judges.

"It's so good to see you," Benson said. He pulled away from their hug to put an arm around a beautiful blonde woman who had followed him across the room. "This is my wife, Rachel."

Bess shook Rachel's hand and returned the smile of the younger woman.

"I've heard quite a bit about you," Rachel said, her smile growing larger as she spoke. "Benson wasn't sure he wanted to come to the reunion until he heard that you were going to be here."

Bess' eyes went wide in surprise. Benson hadn't been popular like Gen, but she had always thought he was well-liked and would have plenty of reasons to get together with his old classmates.

"I don't know if you know this, Mrs. W,"—Benson used the nickname he'd started using, which had caught on, leading many of her male students to call her the same—"But I went into law because of you."

Bess cocked her head, unsure of how she could have done that.

"When I started my senior year, I still didn't know what I wanted to do after high school. Because of my overachieving ways, that scared me to death."

Bess chuckled. She'd taught this class when they'd been seniors, several as AP students, and even though most of them had no idea what they wanted to do or be when they grew up, she could imagine a student like Benson wouldn't have been okay with that.

Rachel laughed along with Bess as Benson continued. "We did that project on *The Crucible*."

Bess nodded. She remembered it well. And although she remembered Benson's project specifically, she didn't remember it as being extraordinary or having anything to do with law.

"I had always assumed I wanted to do something with English," Benson said.

"You were good at it," Bess responded.

"But I hated *The Crucible*."

Bess laughed. She had not expected the story to take this turn.

"How could I do something with English for the rest of my life if I hated one of the greatest pieces of literature?" Benson asked.

"How?" Rachel said in a teasing tone that Benson smiled at.

"Anyway, I had to dig deep, and I realized I like truth and justice. Those were the things in English that made me so engaged in the subject."

"And what better way to follow truth and justice than law," Bess said with a wide smile. She had no idea she'd had a lifelong impact on any of these students, and the thought acted as a balm on her troubled heart.

"Not according to all the jokes. But in reality, yes," Benson said with a grin.

"Thank you for sharing that with me, Benson," Bess said before she heard Roy call Benson's name.

"My fans await, but thanks again, Mrs. W," Benson said before leading his wife toward a group of men who stood near the windows.

"Oh, thank goodness." Eveline turned around and took notice of Bess. "Would you mind terribly helping us out?" Eveline asked.

Bess shook her head. It was as if Eveline had read her mind. "I'd love to," Bess said, and Eveline breathed a sigh of relief before instructing Bess on how the meal was supposed to go. Eveline had been hoping to leave the sign-in table early enough to take care of that as well, but people were still coming in and the meal needed to begin.

As Bess hurried to the kitchen to do as she'd been asked, thoughts of her husband and his infidelity were pushed to the borders of her mind. Even if the reprieve from the knot in her stomach accompanied by constant nausea was only temporary, Bess would take it.

TWO

"OLIVIA PENN, or I guess it's Olivia Birmingham now, right?" Eveline greeted as Olivia came to the sign-in desk at her reunion alone. She'd expected her husband to be back from Seattle hours before, but he was running late. Again.

"Yes, good to see you, Eveline," Olivia said in the calm voice she'd mastered over the years. If she could keep her surface sweet and docile, no one ever knew the turmoil that was raging in her. That was the way Olivia liked it.

"You look incredible," Eveline gushed as she wrote Olivia's name on a nametag.

Olivia knew she looked good. She made sure of that. Hours in the gym, sessions with her personal stylist, Botox, nails, and many hours in the salon getting the hair on different parts of her body colored, waxed, and blow dried.... Her appearance was in peak form.

"And is Bart ..." Eveline's voice trailed off as she looked around Olivia and saw no one with her. That was the one part of Olivia's appearance she could do nothing about. Bart Birmingham answered to no one, least of all his wife.

"He'll be here soon," Olivia said authoritatively, even though she had no idea where Bart was or when he was going to show up. But what kind of wife would she be if she wasn't sure of Bart's actions?

"We're all looking forward to it," Eveline said, and Olivia fought the sudden urge to turn her smile upside down.

She knew Eveline, of all women, meant nothing by her remark. Eveline was just looking forward to seeing an old classmate, the guy who had been popular and well-liked in high school. But in Olivia's world, women were always after her husband, and often they were able to catch him. Her stomach grew queasy at that reflection, so she moved her thoughts right along. She was good at that.

"And lots of people have been asking about you. So you better get that beautiful booty in there," Eveline said.

Olivia's smile felt a bit more genuine as she turned from the check-in table toward the rest of the room.

The decorations were fairly good considering there needed to be a cheesy element. It was a reunion, after all. The view of the ocean from the picture window caught Olivia's attention, and she found her feet drawing her there of their own accord. She'd always found grounding and solace near water, especially the Salish Sea that surrounded her home on Whisling Island. Tonight she needed that solace more than ever. She couldn't believe Bart was late. He'd promised her he would be there in time for the two of them to come together. Bart didn't make many promises to her anymore, so she'd assumed since he'd made this one, he would keep it. But she should have known he wouldn't care. When was the last time he'd cared?

"Olivia!" Kandy Jones rushed over from where she sat with a few of the other women Olivia had hung out with in high school and gave her a big hug. "It's so good to see you."

Olivia smiled and returned the hug, wishing she could say the same honestly. Kandy had been a sort of frenemy in high school, and she seemed to want to keep that as her role in Olivia's current life as well, making passive aggressive remarks on social media and doing her best to keep Olivia from appearing to have too great of a life. So since Olivia couldn't return her greeting, she smiled instead.

"And where is Bart?" Kandy grinned and winked as if Bart were a prize that Olivia should be showing off.

Bartholomew Birmingham had always been a force of nature. And in the summer before junior year, Bart had caught Olivia in his current and she'd been along for the ride ever since. He charmed everyone he met. While guys wanted to be his best friend, most women ended up wanting him, much to Olivia's dismay.

They'd attended college together, and after that it had only taken a few years for Bart to climb the ranks at the Seattle-based financial planning firm where he worked. At that point, not only was he handsome and charming Bart, he was also successful Bart. Because of that, all of Olivia's friends were sure she'd won the lottery. If they only knew. But they didn't. And they wouldn't. Olivia was sure to keep things that way.

"Running a few minutes behind. You know how things can get at the office," Olivia said as she put a hand on Kandy's arm, and the second woman beamed.

"Yes. Our husbands and their jobs. Can't live with them, can't live without them. Am I right?" Kandy said as she tugged Olivia's arm to twine with hers and led her to the table where she'd been seated. "My husband couldn't make it, and although I wanted to cry, I get it. He's producing a huge movie and just couldn't get away."

Kandy proceeded to name drop many of the Hollywood A-listers who were a part of her husband's movie and then gushed about life in LA. Kandy had left the island as soon as graduation was over to start her career in the movies. She hadn't quite gotten there, but she'd landed the role of wife and acted as if she'd accomplished her greatest dream. Olivia hoped that was the truth. She knew success could hide so many terrible things.

"Look who I brought," Kandy said in a sing-song voice to the women at the table who all gave their greetings to Olivia. Like her, almost all of them were dressed in the best designers, their hair coiffed to perfection. No one in Olivia's high school inner circle wanted this night to go by looking anything less than perfect. It was what they had appeared to be in high school and what they still tried to achieve now. But no one was perfect. Olivia knew because she'd spent her entire life trying, only to come short time and time again.

"Where's Bart?" Sarah and Lynn asked simultaneously, turning to one another as they laughed at their action.

"Work. He'll be here soon," Olivia promised, something she wasn't sure she was going to be able to deliver. She'd assumed this night was as important to Bart as it was to her. It was the only reason she had been sure he would come. If it had been just Olivia's reunion, she knew Bart would have blown it off. If it wasn't an event for Bart or if there wasn't anything in it for him, Olivia's husband didn't make the effort. But this night was for both of them. So why wasn't he here?

Sarah went on to tell the table about the yacht her husband had just bought. She was one of Olivia's classmates who had stayed on the island, and Olivia knew all about the boat.

"Why does she keep calling it a yacht?" Kandy whispered in Olivia's ear. "She does realize what they got is practically a fishing boat. It's just missing the oars." Kandy laughed, and Olivia knew she wanted Olivia to giggle along at the joke she'd made at the expense of their friend, but Olivia couldn't do it. She was too tired and old to be a part of these petty games anymore. Even back in high school they'd been juvenile.

Olivia gave Kandy a tight smile before asking Lynn where she'd gotten her dress.

"A boutique in Seattle," Lynn said with a sweet smile. She'd been the only one of them to be above all the gossip and pettiness. Olivia had admired and been somewhat jealous of that ever since high school.

Lynn sat next to her husband, a man who was a bit on the rotund side and had a receding hairline. But what Olivia noticed most was the way he couldn't keep his eyes off his wife.

"You'll have to give me the name of that place," Olivia said, wishing she was sitting closer to Lynn instead of across the table.

Lynn wasn't the only one accompanied by her husband. Sarah sat whispering to hers, and he sat next to their last friend, Patty's, newest boyfriend. Patty had been a serial dater in high school and hadn't seemed to change her ways. The woman didn't seem ready to settle down, even though the rest of their friend group were all married.

"Can you believe the pounds Lynn has put on?" Kandy whispered again. "I mean, nowhere near as many as her husband, but come on. It's like she doesn't even care about her appearance."

Olivia scooted away from Kandy, hoping the woman got her message. Olivia was done with the gossiping. What she wanted to do was fight for Lynn—the woman had barely put on weight, especially considering she'd had four children—but Olivia knew that her saying anything would only result in Kandy's remarks becoming loud enough to get back to Lynn. That wouldn't be fair to the sweet woman who wouldn't hurt a fly.

Dinner was announced, and Olivia went to the buffet station, along with the rest of her group. She filled her plate with salmon, fresh salad, and an array of shellfish that Whisling was famous for before sitting back down and enjoying the delicious fare.

Olivia was almost finished with her dinner when a commotion happened near the door. She didn't even need to turn to know that her husband had arrived. The whisperings that began, the way all heads were turning, it was what Bart did. It was what he had always done, what had drawn Olivia in. But now, being so close to the person everyone assumed was a light ... Olivia felt like she'd been burned time after time. Because Bart didn't ever dull his light so that the people around him could shine for themselves. Bart was always the best and brightest; the rest of the world just had to deal with that.

"Oh, it's Bart," Kandy said, and Olivia tried to ignore the way Kandy tugged down on her bodice so that her chest nearly popped out of the tight, red dress.

Bart charmed Eveline, it was easy to see the shining in her eyes even from Olivia's table, and then moved on to talk to a group of men who were standing near the bar.

"Call him over," Kandy demanded Olivia, but Olivia shook her head. She wasn't about to let all of her classmates see just how little Bart cared about what Olivia wanted. He would turn at her call and give her the slight narrowing of his eyes he always did when she did something he didn't approve of. Then he would turn back to whomever he wanted to talk to. One thing Olivia had learned over the years? Bart only did what he wanted to do.

Olivia turned back to her former friends, trying to restart the conversation by asking Patty and her boyfriend how they'd met. She worked hard to ignore the fact that her husband hadn't even acknowledged that she was in the room, even though she hadn't seen him in nearly two weeks.

Bart worked and lived in Seattle. He came home on most weekends, but he'd hardly even done that over the past few months. Olivia had speculated about many things that could be keeping him in the city, and she'd narrowed it down to one. A woman. It was always a woman for Bart. She swallowed back her revulsion and smiled at those around her.

The conversation at the table continued for a few more minutes before Kandy said, "He's looking around. I bet he's trying to find you. Call him over."

Olivia realized that her friend had kept an eye on her husband that whole time, and Olivia refused to wonder why.

"The room isn't very big. He'll make his way over soon, I'm sure," Olivia said. But she wasn't sure. She could never be sure of anything when it came to her husband.

"So your oldest is nine?" Lynn asked Olivia, and Olivia shot her a grateful smile.

"Yes. Rachel. And Pearl is seven." Olivia spoke with great pride about the one part of her life that could always make her genuinely happy.

"I've seen the pictures on Facebook. They are gorgeous," Lynn gushed.

"Well of course they are. Have you seen their parents?" Kandy said before turning back to Bart.

"Bart! Bart!" she yelled, apparently not willing to wait for Olivia's plan to pan out.

Bart looked up from the conversation he was having with Dean Haskell, his best friend from high school. The two had grown apart over the years since Dean left the island for Portland after high school, but Olivia had heard at the salon earlier that day that Dean had made it back for the reunion. From the rumors, Dean had done just as well for himself as Bart, and no one was surprised. But of course, since Bart was the sun and everyone else was lucky to just be the stars around him, Dean wasn't getting nearly the attention Bart was.

Bart said something to Dean, and Dean looked over to them,

his eyes making contact with Olivia's before quickly looking away. Dean nodded, and Bart made his way across the room, taking the open seat next to Kandy instead of the one next to Olivia.

Olivia felt her cheeks burn red, and she willed the heat to go away. It did, Olivia had honed her emotions well over the years, but not before Kandy caught a glimpse.

Kandy grinned as she turned to Bart and put a hand on his, looking into his eyes. Kandy had always had a thing for Bart in high school; she had been less than thrilled when Bart had chosen Olivia. But who was Bart choosing that day? Olivia knew it wasn't her.

"We've been waiting all night for you to show up," Kandy said as she leaned into Bart, and out of the corner of her eye, Olivia saw Lynn's eyes go wide. Olivia wished she could be shocked. But she'd seen this exact scene too many times.

"Have you?" Bart said, his voice going low in a way that used to make Olivia's stomach warm. Now she just wanted to leave.

Even from her spot two seats away, Olivia got a whiff of the sour smell of alcohol on her husband's breath and wished she could blame his behavior on his drinking. But he would have behaved this way regardless.

Olivia was a little surprised to find him so deep in the cups —Bart usually wasn't a huge drinker—but he must have imbibed even before coming to the reunion because he hadn't had time to drink more than the glass he was carrying with him since he'd gotten there.

"I think I saw Mrs. Wilder over by the buffet station and didn't get a chance to say hi," Lynn said loudly, even shaking the table as she stood. Olivia was sure it was an attempt to pull Bart and Kandy apart.

But Lynn didn't know Bart. Even realizing they had an audience would do nothing to shame him. Lynn gave Olivia a parting look full of sadness before she left for the buffet to talk to Mrs. Wilder.

Olivia felt tears prick her eyes. It wasn't because of the attention she was lacking or even what Kandy was receiving that made her feel emotional. She was used to that. But how could Bart do this here? In front of all of their friends. It was one thing for him to have his mistresses in the city. Away from Olivia and her children. She could try to ignore it and maintain her life. But right now Bart wasn't just disregarding her, he was disrespecting her.

"Kandy, why don't you tell Bart all about your husband's latest movie?" Olivia said, knowing the only way to get Bart to walk away from a woman who was interested in him. He may have no respect for his own vows and marriage, but he didn't interact with married women. Olivia was pretty sure his actions were purely selfish; Bart didn't want to deal with the mess that ruining a relationship would create and feared the man on the other end. But it was his chastity line. If one could call it that.

"Your husband?" Bart said as he sat back, doing exactly as Olivia had assumed. Olivia knew Bart kept up with no one on social media, so he'd have no idea Kandy had married a big shot Hollywood exec a few years before. Some found Bart's lack of an online presence mysterious. Olivia knew it was only because Bart didn't care.

Kandy shot a tight smile at Olivia before turning back to Bart. She was flirting with Olivia's husband, and somehow Kandy was the one who was allowed to be upset that Olivia had gotten in her way? Olivia felt the urge to hit something ... hard.... But instead she clenched and unclenched her fists beneath the tablecloth and then searched the room for something better. Anything would do.

Lynn and her husband had left with Patty and her boyfriend trailing behind them—everyone had loved Mrs.

Wilder—so only Sarah and her husband and Kandy and Bart remained at the table. Sarah was on her fifth glass of wine since Olivia had sat down, so she was almost certain there wouldn't be much of a coherent conversation happening with Sarah for the rest of the night. And Olivia definitely didn't want to be with Kandy and the man who had chosen to sit by her instead of his wife.

Feeling completely trapped, Olivia stood. She felt Bart's eyes on her. She'd finally gotten his attention, and some sick part of her was thrilled. She was so used to being ignored by the man who had promised to cherish her that even his looking at her was more than she usually ever got.

"Did you need something, Olivia?" Bart asked.

To some those might sound like the words of a doting husband making sure his wife had everything she needed. But Olivia knew the truth. He was telling her to sit down and go back to being invisible. He'd come to her table, and she wasn't going to leave before he did. Bart always did the leaving.

But frustration, which Olivia had long since assumed died along with most of the other emotions she used to feel, bubbled up within her belly. Why should she give into Bart's demand when he gave her nothing?

"I'll take care of it." Olivia defied Brad for the first time in years, and Bart's eyes narrowed, giving her the exact look she knew he would. But suddenly Olivia didn't care. She was sure Bart would be on the next ferry back to Seattle so early tomorrow morning that he might not even see his children. If he could do as he pleased, so should she. At least once she should be able to get her way.

Olivia began to walk and realized she had no plan. She'd just wanted to leave her table. She could always go to the bathroom, but that wouldn't stick it to Bart nearly the way she wanted to.

She spotted Gen sitting with her husband Levi and knew she'd find safe haven there. Gen hadn't been best friends with Olivia in high school, but Gen had been known and liked by everyone—Olivia included. And over the years their acquaintance had grown since Gen owned the salon where Olivia went.

Olivia could feel Bart's eyes on her as she moved a few tables over and sat with her back facing Kandy and Bart.

"Olivia," Gen said happily.

Olivia sighed a small breath of relief that Gen wasn't going to turn her away. She knew that wasn't going to be the case, but she was so on edge about defying her husband that she'd been worried that every part of her tiny plan was going to fail. But it hadn't. She'd made it, and she was fine.

"I love how bright we went today," Gen said as she took ahold of a few strands of Olivia's hair and examined them. "Everyone's been asking me for white blonde, and although I love it, I'm kind of getting bored of it. I'm sure once the women on the island see your hair I'll be getting plenty of requests for a brighter blonde."

Olivia looked over at Gen's hair, which was a dark purply red that day. Gen often experimented with her hair color but usually landed in the red family. It made sense considering her natural hair color was a deep auburn.

"If I could pull off your color, I would've made the leap," Olivia said, and Gen laughed.

"Isn't she gorgeous?" Levi stopped his conversation with a guy Olivia didn't recognize to interject before going back to his conversation. Was that what husbands were supposed to do? Gen shot a sassy smile at her husband before turning back to Olivia.

"Oh, you could." Gen's words pulled Olivia away from her own thoughts. "You, my dear gorgeous woman, can pull off anything."

Olivia knew that was far from the truth but kept her mouth shut. Her appearance of perfection only worked if Olivia didn't tell them the truth.

Loud laughter caused Olivia to turn, and she saw that Bart had moved on from Kandy and was now conversing with a group of guys Olivia hadn't ever liked. Because Whisling High was so small, their school's dynamic was different than most. There were no football players or cheerleaders. Whisling boasted a small basketball team that never did very well, so as far as jocks, there weren't many. But that didn't keep some of them from fulfilling the stereotype of having loud mouths and being bullies. And that was the very group Bart was choosing to converse with. They all looked like they had overindulged that evening, if the redness of their faces and their proximity to the bar said anything.

Olivia fought the urge to roll her eyes at Bart's antics. If interacting with a bunch of idiots was her punishment for defying him, she figured she'd gotten off easy.

She did notice that, once again, Bart's glass was full. She saw him chug it down before getting a refill at the bar right next to him. Bart didn't often drink heavily, and Olivia wondered what had happened to make him do so that night. She figured she would never find out. Bart didn't confide in his wife.

"They're charming," Gen said, making Olivia realize Gen was also watching the men with Bart. Right at that moment, Ryan, one of Bart's conversation partners, puffed up his chest and then hit it hard, causing all of the men to laugh again.

Olivia nodded, frustrated that her husband was acting so out of character. But she figured one night of his childish antics wouldn't ruin the perception of perfection she'd spent their entire married life building.

"It's nice to see Bart home though," Gen said, her voice a little too upbeat.

Is it? Olivia wanted to say, but she settled for, "It is. He works so hard."

Gen nodded.

"But she's so hot," Ryan said, loudly enough for Olivia and much of the room to turn his way.

When Olivia looked at the group of men with her husband, she realized all eyes were on her. She schooled her features, unsure of how to proceed with her perceived emotions until she knew more of what was going on.

Ryan looked between Olivia and Bart and then laughed. "I guess if you can have her and lots of other women, why wouldn't you?"

Olivia felt the blood leave her face. Had he just ...? She had to have misheard Ryan.

Ryan nudged Bart who met Olivia's eyes, a mean glint in them telling her she hadn't misheard a thing and that he knew exactly what he'd done. This was her world, her island. He was going to escape back to the city in the morning, and she was going to deal with all of the fall out. Not that there would have been much for him to deal with, even if he did stay. But for Olivia and their daughters? He wouldn't do this. He didn't hate her. Did he? And yet, he'd just ruined everything.

Olivia replayed the words in her mind, knowing there was only one thing they could mean.

"Bart, you are the man!" Ryan said loudly as Dean came up to the group and pulled Bart away.

Dean shook his head as he spoke to Bart, and that was all Olivia saw before her eyes filled with tears. She batted them away before looking down at the table. What was she supposed to do now?

"Wait, is Bart cheating on Olivia?" Ryan's wife, Lorena, said as she came up to join the group, her voice just as loud as her husband's. Olivia knew the room was waiting for Ryan's response. They all wanted that confirmation.

"Let's get out of here," Olivia heard Gen say as she pulled her up from her chair and helped her to get stable on her feet.

Olivia's stomach roiled. She knew she had to get out of there fast.

"Restroom," Olivia requested, and Gen hurried her that way.

They'd made it to the door of the bathroom when Olivia heard Ryan's response.

"Oh yeah. Big time," he said, and Gen pushed Olivia through the bathroom doors before she heard anything else.

The whole world knew. The secret Olivia had kept for years was out for every ear to hear and every mind to judge.

Olivia rushed to the porcelain throne and lost all of her dinner. How could this have happened? She had worked so hard to never let her secret out. Her poor girls. They couldn't find out like this. She felt her chest tighten. Would they even understand? What was she supposed to tell them? What was she supposed to do?

Olivia sat down on the floor of the restroom, leaned against the wall beside the toilet—something she would have never done before that night—and tried to get some toilet paper to wipe her mouth.

"Here." Gen offered a paper towel, and Olivia cleaned herself up.

"I'm ..." Gen began and then stopped.

Olivia let the silence reign. It was better than the alternative. There were no words for that evening.

"Olivia, do you need anything?" Gen asked softly.

Did she need anything? Heck yes, she did. But where to start?

"Maybe water?" Olivia asked, and Gen nodded.

Olivia heard the door open and Gen say, "Get an 'out of order' sign for the door. People can use the other bathroom. Guard the door until I get back. Make sure no one goes in."

The door closed, and Olivia let her head fall to her knees. What had Bart done?

THREE

"BESS, I NEED YOU," Gen said as Bess held her coat in one hand.

She had been just about to walk out. Rumors of Bart's infidelity had reached her almost immediately, and Bess had already brushed away too many tears that evening. Some for dear, sweet Olivia and many for herself. The distraction of the reunion had only worked for so long. Bess was too tired to stay but not ready to go home. Thankfully, she wouldn't have to face Jon since she'd told him to leave, but going home meant she'd have to face the truth.

"Is everything okay?" Bess asked at the tone of her sister's voice, her own problems falling secondary to whatever was happening to Gen.

"It's Olivia," Gen said.

Bess nodded. "I heard."

"I have her holed up in the bathroom, and I can't ... I have no idea what to say to her, Bess. You're so much better in these kinds of situations," Gen said, holding up a glass of water in her hand. "I'm afraid I won't be able to do much more than this."

Bess felt overcome with exhaustion. She hardly ever denied her sister anything, but this she couldn't do.

"I'm sorry, Gen—" Bess started.

"Bess, her husband just revealed to the world that he's had mistresses for years. According to Levi, he gave those douchebags details. Olivia is hurting and falling apart. She needs more than me," Gen said, her face sullen and her eyes devoid of the light they normally held.

"I'm not sure I'm it. Not tonight. I'm tired and—"

"You on your worst day is better than most of us on our best. Please, Bess?" Gen pleaded, and suddenly Bess couldn't say no. Of all nights, she knew this was one where no one would blame her for being selfish. She could give Gen a small piece of her conversation with Jon that afternoon, and Gen would understand in an instant. But Bess didn't want to. She wasn't ready to say anything, and honestly, maybe more of a distraction would be good for her.

Bess nodded and followed Gen toward the restrooms. Instead of a big room with a number of stalls and sinks, this restaurant had gone with one large room for men and one for women. Bess saw Levi positioned in front of the room for women, standing guard.

"I'm going to grab an 'out of order' sign, and then I'll be right out here if you need me," Levi said to Gen as she and Bess approached the bathroom.

Gen nodded and gave a small smile to her husband before pushing back her shoulders and walking into the room. Bess saw her sister fortifying herself and decided she should do the same. She drew in a deep breath before following Gen.

Bess nearly crumbled at the sight of Olivia curled up into herself on the restroom floor. Olivia was a strong and proud woman. To see her like this was heartbreaking. Olivia looked how Bess felt.

"Here's some water," Gen said as she held out the glass so that it was right next to Olivia's head. "And I brought my sister."

Olivia finally looked up to meet Bess' eyes and then took the glass of water from Gen.

"Thank you," Olivia whispered, and Gen nodded.

Olivia looked from the coat in Bess' hands to her face.

"You were about to leave," she said. "I'm sorry. I'll be fine." Olivia tried to get up but slid back down as if her legs weren't quite strong enough to carry her slight weight.

"You aren't fine, and that's okay," Gen said as she crouched down beside Olivia.

"It's not okay." Tears began to overflow from Olivia's eyes and down her cheeks. "Nothing is okay," she whispered.

Gen nodded but then looked up to Bess for help.

The first thing Bess knew Olivia needed was to stand back up. Being crumpled on the ground helped no one.

Bess stepped forward and took the glass from Olivia before handing it to Gen. She then took Olivia's hands and pulled her up to her feet before letting Olivia fall into her. Olivia was nearly half a foot taller than Bess' five foot three, but she was almost feather light as she leaned much of her weight on Bess. Bess wondered when the last time was that Olivia had eaten a good meal.

"I can't believe I still trusted him. After all he'd done, I thought he'd keep my secret. Our secret," Olivia said into Bess' shoulder as she leaned on her.

"This isn't on you, Olivia," Gen said, her voice so strong Bess couldn't see how Olivia wouldn't believe her.

"Isn't it?" Olivia paused and then took a deep breath before saying, "He slept with one of my bridesmaids on the night before our wedding. I'd thought it would be romantic to spend the night apart, and that's how he spent the time without me."

Bess felt her heart clench, wanting to crumble right along

with Olivia but knowing she couldn't. What kind of monster had Olivia married?

There was a soft knock at the door, and Gen opened it wide enough to pull in three chairs and then closed it again.

Bess carefully sat Olivia in one of the chairs and then took her own seat next to Gen.

"He promised it was a one-time thing." Olivia held on to the edge of her chair and looked down at her black stiletto heels as she said the words as if she were ashamed. "I was outraged and sent my bridesmaid away. She had to be the problem, right? Bart loved me. So I went through with the wedding, and here I am today. Eight mistresses later. I might have missed a few in there, but Bart stopped hiding them about a year into our marriage, so they weren't hard to keep track of."

Bess didn't realize her heart could break any more after Jon's revelation, but this was doing it.

"He kept it quiet from everyone here in my world, and I let him live the way he wanted. I told myself it was okay. He was a good father when he was at home. He cared about the girls, and he cared about me. How could I say that about the same man who'd cheated on me countless times? So how can I blame anyone for my situation but myself? I knew. When I screamed at Meg to get away from me and my wedding and that I never wanted to hear from her again, I knew. Meg wasn't the first—I'd had my suspicions before her. She was just the first I caught. And she definitely wasn't the last. But because I knew and married him—"

"You don't deserve this," Gen said adamantly, and Bess couldn't agree more. She could understand how Olivia would think things were her fault, though. All too easily. Hadn't her first thought when Jon had revealed his affair—Bess felt sick to her stomach just thinking the word in association with her husband—been to wonder what she had done wrong? So even though Olivia was so wrong in blaming herself, Bess could understand why ... and how.

"Don't I?" Olivia whispered as she looked up to meet Gen's eyes.

"No, you don't," Bess said firmly. "You were about to get married. Walking away from Bart in that moment would mean calling off a huge event, sending relatives home, losing deposits on flowers, a church, food. You were young, and that seemed impossible, didn't it?"

Olivia nodded, her eyes full of gratitude.

"You had faith in the man who had told you he loved you. You had hope for a better tomorrow than today. That isn't a crime," Bess said softly because she knew the feeling all too well. Isn't that how she still felt about Jon? Even while she was hating him?

"And then I only fell in deeper. We were married, then we had a child, then two. Our house, everything in our lives is so intertwined. How do I even begin to pull myself out?"

Bess nodded. She understood completely.

"So I guess even though my faith and hope wasn't a crime, it didn't help me either. I married a man who cares more for himself than for anyone else and ... I know two women like you couldn't understand this. You both are too sweet and good." Olivia's voice broke.

"Too good and sweet? Oh, Olivia, I think you need to really get to know me," Gen said, and Olivia laughed. It was short, but she'd been able to find humor. That had to be a good step forward. "But we all have our things. We've all committed our own crimes." Bess felt her eyes go wide. What did Gen mean by that? She and Levi seemed so solid.

But now wasn't the time to go into their own troubles, even Bess' recent ones that were so similar to Olivia's and yet so different. Poor Olivia had to be their focus.

"What do you want to do?" Bess asked as she tried to gather her exploded emotions. Now wasn't the time to share or focus on her own life crumbling around her.

"I can't go back, can I?" Olivia said. "Now that everyone knows."

Olivia looked from Gen to Bess, and Bess wasn't sure what Olivia was seeing. Bess was working hard to keep a straight face devoid of emotion since so much of what she was feeling had more to do with her situation than Olivia's.

"Do you think I'm a fool for caring more about his affairs now that it's out for everyone to know? I should have already cared, right?"

"We aren't in any position to judge," Gen said softly. "And no one can say what you should do because you are the one who has to deal with the consequences."

Olivia stared at Gen before shaking her head. "I'm such a mess. Here I was trying to keep my mask in place for so long that I didn't even care to try to clean up what was happening behind it. Now that all is revealed ... I don't even have real friends to help me through this." Olivia looked at Bess and Gen before adding, "I mean, you both are wonderful, but you shouldn't have to be here. You were the best English teacher I ever had, and we both know how I feel about the magic you work on my hair, Gen, but shouldn't I have a best friend who is here with me to clean up the pieces of my life? I don't because I pushed everyone so far away so that they wouldn't get close enough to see my mess. Am I even making sense?"

Bess nodded as Gen said, "Perfect sense. But we're here now. If you need us."

Olivia looked up at Gen and then at Bess with tears glittering in her eyes.

"Thank you," she whispered as Bess tried to smile in return

because it seemed to be what Olivia needed. But the emotions in the room were overpowering, to say the least.

"I think I have to go home with Bart," Olivia said, sitting up straight in her seat. "I have to talk to him."

Bess nodded, even though she wasn't sure she agreed with Olivia's plan. But she agreed with Gen that Olivia had to make her own decisions tonight and every other night if she was the one living with the consequences.

Olivia went to the mirror and began swiping at the mascara under her eyes. Gen wet a paper towel and handed it to Olivia so that she was better able to wipe her messed up makeup away.

"We have two children together," Olivia said, more to herself than the other women in the room.

Bess watched Olivia and wondered how many times she'd endured this same scenario, knowing her husband had been unfaithful and working hard to pick up the pieces of her life. Bess couldn't do it. She wouldn't do it. Even for her children. Jon needed to leave, and Bess needed to move on, on her own. Even just thinking the thought sent shivers through her—she couldn't begin to comprehend how she would live alone after being part of a pair for the last thirty years—but she couldn't be Olivia. She couldn't find herself five, ten, twenty years down the line still making excuses for her husband. Jon had said it was a one-time thing, and he had apologized, practically groveled for Bess' forgiveness. So maybe her situation was different. But the way she felt wasn't. She felt broken and afraid, and she couldn't just take Jon back so that she'd no longer feel that way. She needed to heal herself. Without Jon. They had to separate.

"Thank you both ... for everything." Olivia turned away from the mirror to look at Bess and Gen.

Gen nodded as Bess said, "Of course."

Olivia nodded in return and then looked at the door. She

drew in a deep breath and left the bathroom to face her new future.

Gen leaned her head on Bess' shoulder as the door shut behind Olivia.

"I couldn't have done this alone. Thank you, Bess," Gen said.

And although Bess still didn't feel any better about her own life, she was glad she had come back. Seeing Olivia's situation firsthand had forced Bess to face the reality of her much needed decisions. Bess now knew how she wanted to proceed, at least for the time being.

"I love you, Gen," Bess said, grateful she had one steady relationship in her life she could continue to count on.

"Forever and ever, Bess," Gen responded in the way she had until she was about thirteen anytime anyone had told her they loved her.

Seeing Olivia all alone made Bess all the more grateful for Gen. Bess was sure the road ahead of her would be messy, but as soon as she let Gen in, she knew her sister would always be by her side. Bess would never be alone.

BESS KNEW she had to tell her family what was going on. It had been a week since Jon had moved out. He was staying at a hotel close to the university, something he'd done on occasion in the past when he'd been working on writing textbooks, so it wasn't completely out of the norm. But people would begin to question things if Bess didn't let Jon come home soon. And she wasn't ready for that.

She'd come home the night of the reunion to an empty home and king-sized bed, crying herself to sleep. She awoke with puffy eyes, a quick reminder of what her life had become, and started crying again. After about an hour of that, she was done and felt anger bubble within her belly. The anger got her moving, and she threw everything out of Jon's side of their closet into the guest room. All of his dress shirts and pants were thrown in a wrinkled mess on the blue duvet of the guest bed, and Bess didn't even care that the underwear and socks she'd painstakingly washed, dried, and folded were all over the beige carpet. It wasn't quite the dramatic move that she'd seen on the movies where women gave away or burned the clothes of the men who'd wronged them, but it was more Bess' style. She then put everything he'd left behind in their bathroom and bedroom, including his pillow, into a few garbage bags and put them all in the guest room. The purging had helped her to get through the anger, and then she went back to crying in her emptier bedroom.

The cycle continued for a week, but Bess was finally done. She was ready to move on to the next step. She just wished she knew what the next step was. What she did know was that she wanted to tell Gen and her best friend, Deb, the truth. And then maybe talk to her kids. They needed to be told sooner rather than later that their father had moved out.

Deb had already been planning to come over in about an hour. She'd been out of town for the last week and a half and needed to check in with her best friend, so Bess could tell her everything then. Bess loved having a good plan. But before Deb, she needed to speak to Gen.

She'd told both her best friend and sister she'd been sick, the only way to get them to keep from calling and visiting for so long, but she was now ready to talk. Bess guessed maybe that was the next step she was supposed to take?

She called Gen, quick to get to the point, and Gen listened quietly as Bess told her what Jon had done and how Bess had reacted.

"So he moved out?" Gen asked.

"Because I asked him to," Bess said as she opened and shut her kitchen cabinets, needing to do something but unable to focus on any one task enough to actually get anything done.

Gen was quiet on the other side of the line.

"How are you, Bess? Really."

"I don't know," Bess said honestly as she let the last cabinet shut and moved to sit at her kitchen island. Bess drew along the tan pattern of her white quartz countertops as she sat on a stool, waiting for Gen to respond.

"What do you need?" Gen asked, and Bess looked around at the kitchen where Jon had told her what he had done. Her stomach clenched again, and it was like no time had passed.

"Everything," Bess whispered as a tear rolled down her cheek. How did she still have anything left to cry?

"Bess," Gen whispered, and Bess heard her sister sob before stifling it. Bess knew Gen was trying to be strong for her sake. But Gen loved Jon almost like a brother. No, she loved him just like a brother. Jon had been in Gen's life since she was six.

Bess realized she needed to end this call and let Gen grieve. Especially because she had no answers for her sister. Bess had no idea where she was going to go from there. She hadn't completely written her husband off. He was still her husband and, despite all of the sadness, anger, and pain, somewhere deep down Bess loved Jon. She kind of hated herself for it.

"I'm so sorry," Gen said, adding, "If I had known, I never would have asked you for your help with Olivia."

"That was good for me." Bess thought about the way she'd been able to sift through her life so much better when she'd been in that bathroom. Things were a lot less clear now here in the kitchen, living room, and bedroom she'd shared with Jon.

Gen seemed unsure of what to say next, and Bess didn't blame her. How could they end this call with so much still so wrong? They were used to solving problems together, but this wasn't something they could solve in a day ... or maybe ever.

"I love you, Gen." Bess said the words she hoped her sister would really hear. Despite the ragged feeling in her chest and her heart, she had to protect her baby sister from as much of it as she could. Even if Bess was the one enduring it.

"Love you, Bess," Gen said, and Bess decided to just hang up. There was nothing more to do or say.

Exhausted after the call, Bess moved to the living room to sit on her perfect oversized brown couch. As she sat and stared out of the enormous white framed window that looked over her cove, the memory of the hours she'd poured into researching and sitting on hundreds of couches before she'd settled on this one came to mind. Maybe that had been her problem? Jon had been her first serious boyfriend. She'd taken more time and effort to find the perfect brown couch to fit into her living room than a man for her life.

Bess knew she still had to tell her children, but after her call with Gen, she didn't know if she had it in her. Her three kids had all settled in Seattle, at least for the time being, and often came home for Sunday dinner. Bess wished they were even closer but made do with what she had. Maybe it would be best to tell them in person? Sunday was the next day, and she decided that felt right. She'd make them all their favorite foods in an effort to dull the blow that was sure to hit them when their father didn't join them for the meal. Would they blame Bess? Would they be angry with Jon? Bess decided those were worries for a different day and tried to focus on planning a menu. Cooking a big meal was exactly what Bess needed.

Knowing what to make for Stephen, her oldest, was easy. Stephen had adored chicken parmesan from the womb. Bess had craved it at least once a week while pregnant and then had to continue making it nearly as often for most of Stephen's life.

Lindsey was a little bit harder since she wasn't as easily won over by food as her brothers. Bess knew it wasn't the savory foods that comforted her daughter but rather desserts. Specifically, chocolate trifle. It was delicious and relatively easy to make. And then sweet James. Her two boys were often opposites in many things. Although they both loved to eat, where Stephen always opted for pasta and red sauce, James had always been a fan of bread and butter sauces. James loved a good shrimp scampi that Bess could serve with a loaf of crusty bread, and her youngest would be thrilled. Hopefully the food would help because she knew they would all take the news hard. Especially Stephen. He'd always been his father's little buddy.

"Knock, knock." The voice Bess had been expecting called out as Deb entered through Bess' front door.

Bess waited for her best friend to find her, unsure of what she should say or do. This had been the longest in years that Bess had gone without seeing or speaking to Deb. Deb had been at an art show in Portland, displaying some of her most recent paintings, and it was only because of that distance that Bess had been able to keep what Jon had done to her a secret from Deb for a week. Telling Deb she'd been sick had been the only way to keep their communication to just texting. And if Deb hadn't been gone, Bess wasn't sure she would have been able to keep this from Deb for so long. But if Bess was going to be honest with herself, this time alone had been good for her. She wasn't ready to move on or whatever she was supposed to do now, but she didn't feel as fragile as she had a week before. She'd cooked and cooked some more, a pastime that had always been a source of joy. She felt like this time with herself had been what she'd needed to discover her own inner voice and some of the desires she'd put away in order to care for her children and Jon.

"Are you feeling better?" Deb asked as she walked into the living room with a piece of lasagna she must have already snagged from Bess' refrigerator. Deb had never been shy about eating cold anything.

Bess nodded but then stopped when she realized that was the truth. She was feeling better. Not in the way Deb was asking, but Bess was in a better place today than she had been last week. That had to say something, didn't it?

"Something is different," Deb said as she looked around the room and then dug her fork into the pasta and congealed cheese that Bess itched to take from her and nuke for a few minutes. The dish would be so much better that way.

"What?" Bess asked. Besides her bedroom and the guest room, there weren't any other changes Bess had made to the home. Other than the fridge full of leftovers, since Bess had been cooking up a storm and could only eat so much.

"Where's Jon?" Deb asked.

Bess had known she was going to have to tell her best friend that her husband had moved out, but she hadn't realized Deb would figure it out on her own.

"It's the middle of the day, Deb," Bess said, now a little curious as to how Deb had figured it out. Or had she?

"Your eyes are red and puffy, and I can't smell his cologne," Deb said as she narrowed her eyes on Bess as if looking for more.

"Was his cologne that strong?" Bess asked.

"My nineteen-year-old wears less body spray than Jon does," Deb said with a chuckle and then stopped. "So why doesn't it smell like Jon around here?"

Bess swallowed as she prepared to tell yet another person about what had happened. She knew this was what Jon had done, so why did it feel as if she was telling people about her own failure?

"Jon moved out."

Deb sat on the couch next to Bess and set her lasagna on the round coffee table. She put a hand on Bess' leg as she urged her to go on.

Bess drew in a deep breath. "Because I asked him to."

Deb nodded once and then waited for more.

"He slept with one of his aides," Bess said and felt tears well up in her eyes once again. It never got easier to say. Her husband, the man she'd adored for more than half her life, had cheated on her. Had cheated her. Because that's what it really was. Due to Jon's actions, Bess was now cheated out of a life she'd assumed was hers. Her future, when she finally figured out what it would be, would forever be altered.

Bess watched Deb's jaw go tight. She knew her friend wouldn't take the news well.

"His aide? Really? Could the guy be any more cliché?" Deb asked, and Bess shrugged.

Since they were talking about clichés, what about Bess? She was the woman who'd put her entire life on hold to take care of a man. She felt nearly as involved in his career as he was. She'd put in late nights, even with young children and babies, to help Jon study for his PHD. She'd quit her job because it was what had made sense for Jon and their little family. But now she was a middle-aged woman with no future options other than going back to the man who had betrayed her.

"Why? Did you ask him why?" Deb asked, and Bess tried not to be upset at her friend's reaction. She knew Deb felt betrayed as well, but shouldn't she be asking about Bess?

"No. I don't care," Bess said. She didn't want to know how she had failed her husband enough for him to turn to another woman, and Deb sat back, her eyes wide with disbelief.

"You don't care? Well, you should," Deb said.

Why did it feel like Deb was yelling at Bess?

Bess blinked away the last of her tears, and Deb's face fell.

"I'm so sorry, Bess. I reacted in the worst way possible." Deb pulled Bess into a hug and nearly crushed her with the strength of it. "I just ... I don't know how Jon could do this to you. Now, Rich? I could see him doing this in a heartbeat."

Bess gasped that Deb could say that about her husband, but Deb just laughed. "I mean, I'd kill him if he did it, but he's living on the other side of the world. Who's there to keep him in line?" Deb shook her head and turned her attention back to Bess. "Do you want me to kill Jon?"

Bess saw the sincerity in her crazy friend's eyes and knew the woman would do that for her. Deb would do anything for Bess and vice versa.

"I think I'll let him live," Bess said, followed by a sound that was a sob mixed with a laugh.

"Really?" Deb asked as she met Bess' eyes. Bess knew Deb was asking her what she wanted. Deb was ready to do anything.

"He's not a bad person." Bess said the words she'd thought to herself numerous times. It would be so much easier to hate Jon if he was. He'd been so sorry. Or at least seemed so. He said he'd been selfish. That he'd let a flirtatious friendship go too far. Bess wasn't sure how anything went that far. She hadn't even had a private conversation with a man besides her husband since she'd been married.

"Could've fooled me," Deb said under her breath and then turned away from Bess to look at the giant TV Bess had never wanted in her living room. She'd told Jon he could put it up in the den, but Jon had wanted it here. Maybe she should take that down?

"When?" Deb asked, and Bess shrugged.

"You didn't ask him that either?"

"I didn't want any details. He told me more than I wanted to hear already," Bess said.

"You didn't want to know he cheated on you?" Deb asked.

"No." Bess paused, thinking about Olivia. Living in denial

wasn't great either. "Yes, I guess. I mean, I think ... I just wish he'd never done it."

Deb nodded, understanding her best friend.

"Have you spoken to an attorney?" Deb asked, and Bess shook her head. Was that what she should do? Did she want a divorce? The word had always been so foreign to her. Something she would've never turned to. But now? Did this change things? Did it change her?

"You should, Bess. At least know where you stand. I've heard of men getting a jump on things because they aren't as emotionally involved and leaving women with nothing after hiding all of their assets in new accounts. Don't let Jon screw you over twice," Deb said and then stopped.

"I'm so sorry. That was callous," Deb said, and Bess nodded. It was. But this was Deb. She knew her best friend was rough around the edges, but it was part of why Bess loved her.

"But I *am* emotionally involved, Deb. There are so many emotions," Bess said as she felt herself get choked up again. After not feeling them that first day for so long, now all Bess could do was feel. Why couldn't she be stronger? Like Deb. She imagined Deb wouldn't cry at the drop of a hat if this had happened to her.

"I know, Bess. That's why you need me. I'm not. Please let me help you," Deb pleaded.

Was this the kind of help Bess wanted? A part of her brain told her even if she didn't want it, this was what she needed.

"Just talk to an attorney. I dated a guy from Seattle that is a genius with divorce cases. He always wins. He'll just talk to you and give you your options. But for what it's worth, I think you should walk away," Deb said with so much sincerity that Bess couldn't be upset.

"Walk away, Deb? He's been my everything for thirty years. I love him." Bess knew she sounded desperate, but that was what made Deb's way of playing hardball so great for Bess. Deb offset Bess' desperation with so much bluntness that Bess felt a little less desperate arguing her point.

"But does he love you? And can you trust him? A good woman once told me that love without trust is just a hollow shell of the real thing," Deb said softly, repeating the words Bess had told Deb before Deb had married Rich many years before. Bess had no idea her advice had stuck.

"Can't trust be rebuilt?" Bess asked.

Deb shrugged. "Probably. But do you want to rest the fate of everything on a probably? Talk to Doug."

"Doug the divorce attorney," Bess said. "Has a nice ring to it." She chose to joke instead of cry again. A divorce attorney. Was she shying away from the idea because it wasn't right for her or because she was afraid and unwilling to use the ugly D word? If it was the latter, she needed to talk to Doug.

"Give him my information," Bess said with a firmness she didn't know she possessed, and Deb nodded, knowing this wasn't what Bess wanted but what she needed.

"Now can you just hug me?" Bess asked, and Deb pulled her friend into another crushing hug. Bess would have been mortified to ask anyone else for a hug, even Jon before all of this, but with Deb it was different. There was nothing she couldn't say to Deb.

"We'll eat too much of those lovely leftovers in your fridge and then watch that depressing movie where the husband dies, leaving the woman a trail of clues," Deb said from within their hug.

"It's romantic," Bess countered, and Deb nodded.

Bess thought about the movie and how the main character had to pick up the pieces of her life after her husband died. That was what Bess had to do now. She didn't want to, but she had to. No one else would. So how did she begin to pick up those pieces? Figuring out what kind of job she should do seemed like a good start. Bess didn't think she could go back to teaching. The reunion had been fun, but Bess had breathed too many sighs of relief that she was with a group of thirty-somethings instead of a bunch of teens. Bess felt too old to restart a career that took so much out of her. But what kind of career didn't? Especially if she wasn't going back to something she knew.

Just thinking about a job made Bess feel exhausted, and she figured it would be okay to put away those thoughts for the time being. Thankfully, she had a good amount of savings that would provide for her for a very long time. A job was more about filling her time, and right now, her time felt plenty full. Although with what, Bess wasn't sure.

"You know it's going to be okay. Definitely not today and maybe not tomorrow, but it will be," Deb said, and Bess felt her throat get thick with emotion. But she believed Deb. She might have questioned anyone else, but Deb always spoke the truth, even when it was hard. So one day would be better than today. She'd figure everything out one day. And that gave Bess enough strength to pull away from Deb's hug and put on the movie Deb hated so much.

FOUR

DEB RAN HARDER as she thought about what Jon had done to Bess. Dear, sweet Bess. What kind of—Deb ran through a list of names for Jon that Bess would never approve of—could hurt Bess like that? Jon. Deb fought the urge to run down to the ferry, ride across the water, and run right up to that university to give Jon a piece of her mind. But that wasn't her place. This was about Bess. She would do what Bess wanted. Which she had kindly said was for Deb to butt out, something Deb had never been good at.

Deb enjoyed running outside at all times of the year, but something about the January air hitting her lungs made her feel alive. People thought she was crazy to run outside in the middle of winter, but she lived on the beach on an island in the beautiful Puget Sound. How could she not take advantage of the view of the blue gray water, the salty wind whipping at her baggy sweatshirt, or the briny smell of the sea? The only downside was running along the smooth rocks instead of the finer sand beaches, like by Bess' home. But Deb had mastered the skill over the years and now hardly even thought about how she was placing her feet. It had become second nature.

Thinking about Bess' cove brought her thoughts right back to Jon and his infidelity. What if Rich ever did the same to Deb? Deb had to admit she'd had her suspicions over the years. As a pilot, Rich was nearly always traveling. Now that he had his base in London instead of in Seattle, Deb saw less of him than ever. Part of why she'd joked with Bess that she could imagine Rich doing this more than Jon was a weird attempt to help Bess feel better, but also because it was true. And she'd wanted Bess to contradict her. To tell her that Rich was so in love with her that he'd never betray her. But Bess hadn't said that. Not that Deb blamed her. The discussion had been about Bess and Jon, not Deb and Rich.

Rich was handsome and suave, part of what had drawn Deb in in the first place. She'd been well into her career as a flight attendant before she'd met Rich. Deb had had plenty of flirtations with pilots in the past, but she had a job where she spent nearly as many nights away as she did at home. She didn't want her husband to do the same.

Then Rich happened. Deb would never admit it, she liked to tell him she played hard to get, but Rich knocked her right off her heels the minute they met. She'd been substituting for another flight attendant when the handsome pilot had said hi. Deb felt the immediate attraction and, because of that, kept far away from the cockpit at all costs. But the flight had taken them to Rome, a city where Deb had never been, and when the flight attendants got together to explore during their layover, Rich joined them. There was no avoiding him after that, and it was only a matter of two more days before they went on their first date. The rest was history.

So now, two children later and a continent and an ocean apart, here they were. Rich had started trying for a transfer to London when Bailee had started high school. But it had taken three years to get it, and it hadn't seemed fair to move Bailee right before her senior year. So Deb had stayed on Whisling with Bailee, and Rich had taken his dream position in London. Deb had never been on board with the transfer, so she had been happy to stay behind. And although this arrangement couldn't work forever, Deb figured they'd cross that bridge when they had to. She kind of hoped Rich would get London out of his system and come back to Seattle after the year was up. But if he didn't ... Deb wasn't sure she wanted to leave everything she knew on Whisling. This was home. But what kind of a marriage would they have if they lived so far apart indefinitely?

Was the distance making her question Rich or was it the situation with Bess? She remembered a woman who had called claiming to be Rich's lover a few years before, just about the time Rich had put in for his transfer to London. It had been an easy lie to believe since Rich was gone so much, and Deb had flipped. She'd wanted to kill Rich even more than she'd wanted to kill Jon that morning. They'd had a screaming match that would have made the referees in the WWE nervous. But somehow, in the mess, Rich had explained himself. And Deb had calmed down. He'd asked her a few days later why it had been so easy to believe the worst about him. Deb hadn't been able to answer then, and she still couldn't.

But she needed to clear her mind of those kinds of thoughts before Rich came home that evening. He was rarely able to get a long layover in Seattle, but he'd finally arranged one. It would be wonderful to have that time with her husband and for Bailee to have time with her dad. Deb had arranged to take the week off from painting and their oldest, Wes, was even going to come home from college for the weekend. Family time was something they desperately needed, especially for Deb now that she was entertaining such ludicrous thoughts.

Deb turned at the big rock at the end of the beach, the same turning point she always used, and hurried back toward her home. She kept her thoughts on things like the color of the ocean that morning and how she'd blend her paints to get that exact hue, not Bess' situation or worries that Bess might not be the only one needing to figure things out in her marriage.

"Mom!" Bailee called out as Deb opened the white back door of her home that was almost directly off the beach. When they'd first bought the home when Wes was three, the mortgage had been a stretch and, to be honest, a worry. The bungalow home itself was modest with its three bedrooms and bonus room that Deb had turned into a small but useful art studio. However, Deb knew the size didn't matter as much as what was just beyond their backyard. So she begged Rich for this to be the home where they would raise their children, and he gave in. And though the mortgage was a burden for those first few years, after Bailee turned three, Deb went back to painting full time and the amount of cash her sales brought in made their lives fairly comfortable.

"Yes?" Deb asked as she entered the nearly all-white kitchen where Bailee was shoving items into her backpack. Deb had spent hours when they'd first moved in painting everything she could, both inside and outside the home, white. Upkeep was a pain, but the amount of light that appeared in her space because of it was worth it.

"I need you to sign this for school," Bailee instructed as she gave her mother a pen and a paper. Deb knew moments like these wouldn't last forever. Now that Bailee was a senior, the days of signing her permission were numbered. Soon both of her children would be off and living their own lives, not needing Deb's permission or opinion at all. And that scared Deb to her core. It had been hard to let go of Wes, but at least she knew she still had Bailee. But next year? She hated the term "empty nesters." It signified that something was missing that should be there. Bess had dealt with the transition like a champ, but that was just the way Bess took life on. Maybe she'd be able to give Deb a few pointers.

"It's Deb Johnson," Bailee instructed, and Deb realized she was still holding the pen in the air instead of signing the document.

"What is this?" Deb asked belatedly. It was a rookie move to sign something without reading it, but Deb wasn't on top of her game at that moment.

"Just something about our senior projects," Bailee said with a wave of her hand. "Mom, please sign it. I need it today, and I've got to go."

"Hold your horses, Hun," Deb said as she sat on a white barstool at her white marble countertop and read over the form.

"It says you have to turn in a senior project in order to graduate," Deb read.

Bailee nodded. "Dumb, right?" Bailee asked.

"I don't care that you think it's dumb; it must be done," Deb said.

Bailee rolled her eyes but nodded. "I know, Mom. I'm doing it. I just don't want to."

That sounded exactly like something Deb would've said at Bailee's age, and Deb decided to ignore the last statement. As long as Bailee was doing it, Deb didn't need more.

"Great," Deb said as she signed the form and handed it back to Bailee.

"I can't believe you're a senior," Deb breathed.

Bailee shook her head. She was used to her mother reminiscing at the weirdest times. "That I am. I have been for the last four months," Bailee added.

Deb nodded. She knew that. But every day was a step closer to Bailee leaving her home. She knew Bailee looked forward to the day, so she tried to do the same. This was the way things should be. But even if her eighteen-year-old drove her nearly insane, Deb wished she could keep both of her babies with her forever.

"Have a good day, Sweets," Deb said as Bailee headed toward the door that led to the garage.

"I will. Love you, Mom," Bailee said, shutting the door behind her and leaving Deb to wonder if she was going to spill tears over this moment. Bailee might act like she was a woman who no longer needed to be connected to the apron strings, but when she said, "I love you Mom," it took Deb right back to the days when she'd dropped her sweet little pigtailed girl off at kindergarten. Back then Bailee would cry for the entire car ride to school, asking Deb why she had to leave her. She'd always end up telling Deb she loved her before walking into that yellow door with a brave face in place. What Deb wouldn't do to go back to those days.

Deb spent the rest of the morning cleaning in the way she knew Rich liked. Rich was a stickler for neatness and punctuality. Since he'd moved to London, Deb had let their family go lax in both of those areas. But she knew they'd have to step it up before Rich came home.

She picked up a number of items Bailee had left around the house and deposited them in her room. She'd have Bailee pick up her room when she got home from school. She took all of her own items, which she regularly kept on the table or countertop, places Rich wouldn't approve of. He liked things in cabinets and drawers with tabletops clear. It was a concession for him to allow Deb to hang so many of her seascape paintings on the wall, so Deb figured she could give him clear surfaces.

After her home was neat, she did a deep clean of the two bathrooms, dusted every surface, including her art studio which was hardly ever cleaned, and then mopped all of the light pine hardwood floors before vacuuming the areas that had white carpet. She covered and made their bed with the plush, cream duvet Rich preferred—Deb was more of a blanket person but didn't mind sharing a duvet with Rich when he was home—and then went into Wes's room to see that things had been left tidy in her son's space as well. At two, she finally took a break for lunch, eating a turkey sandwich which she dunked in Bess' famous Italian Wedding soup. Then she got a glance at herself in the mirror located in the entryway which could be seen from the kitchen table. she was a mess.

She hurriedly finished up her lunch and then jumped into the shower. Rich wasn't due home for another two hours, but Deb wanted to look her best. That meant shaving her legs and taking more than the ten minutes on her hair and makeup that she typically took.

"I'm home!" Bailee called out after Deb had gotten out of the shower and blow dried her curly hair straight. Rich had always been a fan of her hair being straight.

"Can you clean your room before your father gets home?" Deb called back.

When she didn't get a response, she stepped out of her bathroom and saw that Bailee was in her room, already picking up the things Deb had put in there. Her kids' rooms were two of the few spaces in Deb's home that weren't white. Bailee had opted for a green color palette with her mint duvet and hunter green dresser and matching desk, although Deb had insisted on keeping the walls white.

An answer from Bailee would have been nice, but Deb guessed it was better not to complain since the work was getting done. She had learned that raising a teenage girl was all about picking her battles.

Deb headed back into her gleaming white bathroom to apply her makeup, her least favorite part of getting ready. She remembered a conversation she'd had with Bess a number of years before when Deb had told Bess about her aversion to makeup.

"But isn't it just paint on your face? I assumed as an artist that would be fun," Bess had said, and Deb had honestly never thought of it like that. It had taken her years to come up with an answer to why she disliked putting on makeup so much. She used art as a tool to express what she was feeling, thinking and watching, but makeup wasn't anything like that. It had nothing to do with what was going on inside of Deb and everything to do with her outside. Which Deb had never had much patience for. But she knew it meant a lot to Rich when she dolled herself up, so she did. It was a small sacrifice considering the other concessions one had to make in marriage.

When her makeup was done, Deb headed into her closet and found a blue wrap dress she always felt amazing in. The dress was a bit much for a Thursday evening at home, but she knew Rich would like it.

The one place where Rich wished Deb could excel, which was never going to happen, was in the kitchen. Thankfully, she had a best friend who could outcook the best of them, and Deb's fridge was full of Bess' leftovers that they couldn't finish the night before. So they were going to have some world-class meatball subs made with Bess' homemade meatballs for dinner. It was one of Rich's favorite foods, and all Deb had to do was warm things up and toast some bread. That was the kind of cooking she could handle.

"Oh wow," Rich said as he came into the kitchen through the garage door. Deb felt herself blush at Rich's observation of her, but that lasted for just a moment, thanks to their excited daughter.

"Daddy!" Bailee called out as she came running out of her room and threw her arms around her father's neck, causing him to drop his suitcase in the middle of the kitchen where he stood.

"Bailee boo!" Rich used the nickname Bailee would kill her mother for using, but somehow when Rich said it, Bailee just smiled. Oh to be a dad. "I've missed you."

"I missed you too." Bailee held onto the hug for so long, Deb wondered if they'd done the right thing by staying instead of following Rich to London. But when Rich let go, Bailee grinned at her mom with no longing, just pure joy on her face, and Deb realized all was right in the world. This was exactly as things should be. Well, it would have been nice if Rich could've stayed on Whisling, but that wasn't Deb's choice.

"This smells incredible," Rich said, walking straight to the bubbling meatballs on the stove and completely bypassing his wife. It took Deb a minute, but she realized his *oh wow* had been about the smell, not Deb's appearance.

Deb shook off the hurt—that was no way for them to start this week, and Rich had always loved food—then smiled at her husband.

"Nothing but the best for you," Deb said with a grin.

"Bess?" Rich asked.

Deb pulled a dish towel off the oven door and swatted her husband. "You've gotten quite cheeky in recent months. That's something they say over there, isn't it?" Deb asked.

Rich chuckled. "Something like that," he said.

Deb grinned. It felt good to have Rich home. Complete.

"How's school, Boo?" Rich asked, and that was all the invitation Bailee needed.

"We finally found a location for Prom. I was able to convince Principal Maynard to let us have it in Seattle," Bailee said excitedly. As student body president at a small high school, many responsibilities fell to Bailee.

"Really?" Deb asked from where she was mixing the meatballs on the stove. This was the first she'd heard of these plans.

"Yeah. Isn't it great?" Bailee asked, only sparing a glance for her mother before turning back to Rich.

"The biggest issue with the girls was having to ride the ferry and not messing up their hair. I reminded them that the ferry has an indoor area and told them girls with their hair done for prom would have priority seating." Bailee rolled her eyes as if she couldn't understand this plight of her fellow classmates. "Like hair is something important enough to keep us trapped on the island on our biggest night of high school. Sometimes I feel like the odd man out since I can't wait to get off this rock."

Like her brother, Bailee planned on attending the University of Washington after graduation.

"You could always come to school in London. I hear Imperial College is a good choice," Rich said with a wink that Deb hoped meant he was kidding. Deb would not be okay with her daughter being all the way around the world.

"Um, that would be a definite no," Bailee said with a quick shake of her head. "I want to get off Whisling, but I'll leave the continent hopping to you and mom."

Deb paused stirring the meatballs as she felt the nagging reminder that, if all went to plan, *she* was supposed to be in London next year while her kids stayed here. Her stomach knotted as she turned her attention to the hoagie rolls under the broiler and pulled them out just before they burned. Next year was still many months away. She could figure things out later.

Deb began to place the meatballs on the first roll when Rich said, "No bread for me."

She turned to her husband with a raised eyebrow. Since when did he not eat bread? And how was she supposed to make a meatball sub without bread?

"I've started doing Keto," Rich said as he patted his stomach, which did look a lot leaner.

"Keto? You mean you can't have carbs?" Bailee asked as her

eyes went wide with shock and fear. No carbs was practically a death sentence for Bailee.

"Yes, Bailee, no carbs," Rich said with a laugh. "I'm not super vigilant about it, like I'm sure those meatballs have more sugar than I should have, but I can cut loose about it sometimes."

Deb was still stuck on the fact that her husband had made a huge dietary change and she'd known nothing about it. The Rich who had lived in Seattle would have never chosen willingly to give up carbs. What had London done to him?

"Just put my meatballs between pieces of lettuce. I'm sure it will be great," Rich said as he looked at a still stunned Deb.

That got Deb moving, and she finished Bailee's sub before getting a big piece of lettuce and spooning meatballs on it. This just felt wrong.

"Why?" Deb asked. Rich had always been in shape. He liked to lift weights and ran a few times a week with Deb, but he'd never restricted his diet like this. In fact, he had always been against cutting entire food groups out of his diet. He'd said it wasn't sustainable.

"We're getting older, Deb. Health is important," Rich said.

Deb nodded. She guessed she kind of got that. But was this healthy? She looked at the sad soggy lettuce holding the delicious meatballs. Maybe? She decided it wasn't up to her to judge. Rich had made a change and she should be supportive. Right?

Deb finished making her own sub and then carried the plates over to the table, wondering what other changes her husband had made that she didn't know about. At the beginning of all of this, Deb had thought a year wasn't too long. But now she wasn't sure. Were she and Rich growing apart because of the distance?

DEB STOOD in front of Rich's suitcase, staring at the folded items. Although her husband was a stickler for neatness, his need to be punctual often won out. Because of that, his suitcase was almost always a bunch of clothes haphazardly thrown into each side of the open area with toiletries littered in between. With the number of times Rich had to pack because of his job, he'd always told Deb that it was a waste of time to make sure things were neatly placed. Deb loved to laugh at the oxymoron that her husband's personality was in this specific case.

But this suitcase looked nothing like Rich's normal packing job. She tilted her head, still puzzled by the sight.

"It's the Konmari method," Rich said as he came into their bedroom. Although Deb's back was to the door, she didn't turn around as she waited for Rich to snake his arms around her waist and breathe her in, the same way he did after every trip.

But it didn't happen. Rich came to her side and looked down at the open suitcase on the ground with her.

Deb bit her lip to keep from asking what was wrong because Rich would hate that question. They had been apart for longer than ever. Maybe he needed a day or two to warm back up to things. The solitude of his apartment in London had to be so different than being home with his family.

"Konmari? Like the magic of tidying up?" Deb asked. She'd heard of the woman and the method but had assumed it was too "suburban housewife" for her husband to care about.

"Yeah. Doesn't it sound like something right up my street?" Rich asked, and Deb had to admit it kind of was. Rich did like things neat and clean. But at the same time, it really wasn't. She couldn't imagine Rich sitting down and watching a documentary on how to keep a clean home. Rich liked Deb to do that kind of stuff for him.

"When I have things folded up in her way in my drawers, it makes it so easy to pack," Rich said. Deb saw the end result in the suitcase in front of her, so she couldn't disagree. "Maybe you could do that for my drawers here," Rich suggested, and there it was. Why this felt so wrong. Rich wouldn't have done this for himself. He wanted Deb to do it in Seattle. So who was doing it for him in London?

"My cleaning lady taught me all about it. She even taught me how to pack my dress shirts," Rich said, and Deb breathed a sigh of relief. His cleaning woman. That made so much sense. Deb needed to get off the ledge and forget that things had gone south for Bess. Bess' life wasn't her life.

But thinking about her best friend reminded Deb that she needed to check on her. She planned on going over to Bess' the next day but wanted to get a phone call in that evening.

"Well, maybe since your cleaning lady taught you and not me about this wonderful method, you can be the one to change your drawers here," Deb said sassily. Then she kissed Rich's cheek to soften her statement. She felt him bristle under the contact and almost had to laugh. Rich hated being told what to do.

"I'm going to call Bess," Deb said as she walked out of the room, leaving Rich's suitcase right where it was. She knew Rich had left it out there for her to take care of. But Deb had gone a couple of months without unpacking one of Rich's suitcases, and she liked it. If he could take care of himself in London, he could do it at home.

Deb dialed Bess' number on her cell phone as she grabbed her jacket, shrugging it on as she walked out to her back porch. It was cold but would afford her a little more privacy in case she needed it.

"Deb?" Bess asked when she answered on the second ring. "Didn't Rich just get home? What are you doing calling me?"

Deb shook her head. Of course Bess would be worried about Deb's life instead of wallowing in her own sorrow. The woman was practically a saint, and that thought made Deb want to kill Jon all over again.

"I'm checking in on my dearest and best friend. You've had quite the week."

Deb had been hurt for about a minute after Bess had told her Jon had moved out more than a week before. Why hadn't Bess come to Deb immediately? But then Deb remembered how busy she'd been with her art show in Portland, and then guilt hit her that she'd been unavailable to Bess when she'd needed her most. But Bess had explained to Deb that what Bess had needed was time alone, letting Deb off the guilt hook. According to Bess, it had all worked out the way she'd needed it to. But now that Deb knew, she was going to do everything in her power to help Bess.

"So, how are you? Really. Not the answer you'd give your kids or Gen," Deb said.

Bess chuckled. "Honestly, not too bad considering. I still cry, but only about half the day instead of the entire day."

Deb smiled. She knew that was Bess' attempt at a joke. The woman might be a saint, but she wasn't exactly a comedian. To even be trying to joke at a time like this proved that Bess was better than most normal humans, such as Deb.

"Besides, there are reasons to smile again. Like the Penn's cat came over while I was on the back porch and just settled right in my lap. Oh, and I finally mastered my cannoli recipe."

"Your cannolis were already incredible," Deb said, surprised that Bess had done anything to mess with Deb's favorite dessert of all time. Not just any cannoli was her favorite; Bess' cannolis were.

"Yes, but now they're even better," Bess bragged. Bess was typically too humble to brag, but when it came to her kids and her cooking, all bets were off.

"I'm guessing you have a batch you need me to try then?

Even if you say they're better, I'm not just going to take your word for it," Deb teased as Bess laughed.

Deb knew Bess loved to feed her, especially because Deb was so appreciative of the food. Deb had always loved good food. It was why she continued to run five miles every morning. Although she wasn't quite as svelte as she'd been in her flight attendant days, Deb had to admit the years had been kind to her.

"I can bring some over," Bess offered.

"Only if you want to. But I was planning on coming over tomorrow anyway," Deb said.

Bess stopped her. "No, Deb. Your husband is home for one week. You enjoy him and your kids. I'll still be here after he leaves."

"Bess," Deb said in a way that she knew her best friend would understand. Sure Bess would still be around in a week, but didn't Bess need Deb this week?

"I'm doing okay. I promise. This is my honest answer. I think I'm making some headway in mission 'pick up the pieces of Bess' life.'"

"Oh yeah?" Deb asked, her heart feeling lighter with Bess' declaration. Bess was never far from Deb's mind, especially now.

"Yeah. I'll tell you all about it next week," Bess said.

Deb laughed. "All right. I got it. But you can still drop off some of those cannolis," Deb offered.

This time Bess laughed. "First thing tomorrow."

"Yes! Now I don't have to make breakfast," Deb joked, and Bess chuckled.

"I love you, Bess," Deb said, and Bess returned the sentiment immediately.

Deb hung up and placed her cellphone in her pocket as she looked out onto the water that appeared to be inky under the moonlit sky. She honestly could not imagine what Bess was going through. And yet there she was, making Deb laugh. Deb could only hope she'd deal with such adverse circumstances with the same amount of grace. Who was she kidding? There would be no way.

Deb walked back into her house, checking in on Bailee before heading to her room. It was time to tell Rich about Bess and Jon. Although she and Bess were best friends, over the years the four of them had become a tight knit bunch. Rich should know the truth. She wondered if he'd be as shocked as she was.

She glanced into their bedroom and found no Rich or suitcase. She turned to go into their bathroom, walking through it to get to their walk-in closet. The additional storage space had been another huge selling point of the house for Deb.

Rich sat on the floor, organizing his clothing, and Deb smiled. He still seemed a little upset about Deb leaving him to do the job alone if the hunch of his shoulders told her anything, but he'd soon be over it. Rich had never been able to stay mad at her for too long.

Deb walked into the closet and then dropped to her knees so that she was at eye level with Rich. As an olive branch, she took one of his shirts from a pile and began to fold it in the same way he was folding the others.

"Do you want to know what I just realized?" Deb asked, and Rich looked up from his folding.

"What?" Rich said.

"You have yet to give me a kiss since you came home. A huge oversight on your part," Deb said, and Rich's frown seemed to lessen in severity.

Deb leaned forward and pressed her lips to Rich's frown. She expected him to drop the shirt and pull her into his arms, but even though his lips went soft, indicating his frown was gone, that was all the kiss became before he pulled away. Call her crazy, but Deb had expected more from her husband after two months apart.

Maybe he was still upset that he had to unpack. She guessed that kind of made sense. But why hadn't he kissed her earlier when he'd first walked through the door?

Deb replayed the evening as she folded another shirt and realized Bailee had been around for almost all of their time together, other than when they'd talked about Rich's suitcase. Maybe there hadn't really been a chance to get a good kiss in there?

Or it could be that the distance was messing with Rich. She knew the distance hadn't been their friend and decided maybe a good conversation between husband and wife was what they needed to bring them closer figuratively, and then the literal closeness could come.

"I was just talking to Bess," Deb said as an icebreaker. Rich nodded but didn't say anything. Man, this living apart thing stunk. They didn't even know how to talk to one another anymore. Most of their communication while Rich was gone was over text. They made it a point to call or Facetime once a day, but with the time difference, that usually lasted a few minutes at most. Marriage took more than a couple minute conversation a day to work. At least for her and Rich. They needed to talk about that, but Deb figured telling Rich about Bess and Jon could come first. She knew finding out the truth about their best friends had lit a fire under her to do more for her own marriage, and she hoped Rich would feel the same way.

"Do you want to know how she's doing?" Deb asked.

"I'm guessing just great. Bess is always doing well," Rich said.

Deb shook her head. "Not this time," she said, and Rich paused his folding. "Jon moved out," she continued, and Rich's eyes went wide.

Deb explained what Jon had done, and Rich shook his head.

"Well, dang. If they didn't make it, what hope do the rest of us have," Rich said.

Deb stared at her husband. What did he mean by that?

Rich read her look immediately and added, "I just mean they were practically the perfect couple. If things can go bad for them, it can happen to anyone."

Deb nodded slowly as she considered Rich's words. He was right.

"How's Bess holding up?" Rich asked, his face etched with concern.

"She's okay. Trying to figure out how her life works without Jon," Deb said.

"So she's getting a divorce?" Rich asked.

"Well, yeah. What else can she do?" Deb asked.

"Work it out?" Rich offered.

"Work what out? He cheated. He slept with another woman after making vows of fidelity to Bess."

"Is it that black and white?" Rich asked.

"Of course it is," Deb said, louder than she meant to. But she had to admit she was feeling heated. What was Rich saying?

Rich shrugged after Deb's outburst, and she knew she had effectively shut down their conversation. It wasn't what she'd meant to do, but maybe it was for the best.

"But you were right before," Deb said.

Rich turned to her with a smirk. "Did you just say I was right?"

"Once. For like a split second," Deb said.

Rich chuckled. "So what was I right about?" he asked, still acting smugly.

Deb opted to ignore it. This time. "If it can happen to them, it can happen to anyone. Including us," she said quietly as Rich busied himself with folding. How many shirts did the man have?

"I want to make sure that doesn't happen. Especially now. With this distance. Do you feel what it's doing to us?" she asked.

Rich turned to his drawer to put a pile of shirts in. "What do you mean?" he asked as he placed each shirt in carefully.

"We're growing apart. That kiss was lame," Deb said.

Rich laughed. "I was still mad at you."

"You shouldn't have been."

Rich shook his head at Deb's declaration. But he didn't seem upset anymore, mostly amused and just mildly annoyed.

"We need to communicate better while you're in London. Our calls are as lame as that kiss."

Rich nodded solemnly. "We do."

"And we need to talk about what's going to happen after Bailee graduates," Deb added.

"We do," Rich said again.

"So we're on the same page?" Deb asked.

Rich nodded before leaning in and giving her the kiss she'd been waiting for.

Many minutes later Rich pulled away.

"We are," Rich told a grinning Deb.

FIVE

"MOMMY!" Rachel called out as she came running down the hall. Another call for mommy followed immediately after, this time from Olivia's youngest, Pearl.

Typically, on a morning where Bart had stayed in their home, Olivia would've shushed her children in order to allow her husband to sleep. But today was anything but typical. Bart had, without any prompting from Olivia, stayed in their guest room downstairs, the furthest room from the master bedroom. She would've probably asked him to sleep somewhere other than the place she'd come to think of as her bed, Bart didn't stay on Whisling Island enough for it to feel like theirs anymore, but she would have appreciated the chance to say something. Instead of Bart taking the initiative. But like everything else in her marriage with Bart, things hadn't gone according to *her* plans. Bart was and would always be in control.

"Good morning, sweet girls," Olivia said as she pulled a daughter into each of her arms, and they all fell back into her white pillows together.

Olivia had painstakingly decorated every aspect of their gorgeous home, down to the tiniest of details like the small crystal she kept next to her bed for peace and serenity. Bart had told her she needed to hire a professional—how could a woman like Olivia with no talent in decorating do justice to the home he'd bought for them—but it had been one of the few things in their marriage she'd been adamant about. She wanted their home to be an extension of her, and she didn't think she could find a stranger, no matter how qualified and talented, to do what she could. It was one of the few times she'd felt confident in her own ability, even though Bart had done his best to keep her from feeling so. She'd decorated her bedroom and the surrounding spaces like her closet and sitting room in light purples, to match the crystal, and also bright whites. Between those grounding colors and the sight of the water just outside of her window, she knew the space was a masterpiece. Of course the girls' rooms were both as pink and girly as could be, and she'd gone with nautical greens and blues downstairs. But she'd wanted the place where she sought solace every night to be exactly the way that it was.

"What are you doing?" Pearl asked her mother, and the question didn't surprise Olivia. She was usually up and at 'em at least an hour before her children woke up on Saturday mornings. But last night had drained her, and she'd had little left when she'd awakened before her girls, so she'd opted to stay in bed. But now that her girls were up, life had to go on—including breakfast. Their chef, Patty, had the day off—she was taking a rare personal day—so the girls would have to settle for a breakfast made by Mom.

"She had her big night last night, remember?" Rachel said, startling Olivia into turning to her daughter. Olivia wondered if Rachel had somehow already heard rumors from the night before, but seeing Rachel's big smile, she knew she must have misunderstood her oldest.

She then remembered that the girls had watched as Olivia

had finished getting ready to go to her reunion and had been thrilled that their mother was going on a date with their father. Olivia felt more tears push against her eyes, but she refused to let them be known to her adorable girls. At nine and seven, they deserved a lot more innocence than crying in front of them would offer.

"I did," Olivia said, returning Rachel's smile although it far from indicated what she felt about the night before.

Olivia had tossed and turned in bed for nearly the whole night, wondering what she was going to do. Bart had slipped by telling everyone about his affairs, or had his revelation been intentional? He had been drinking more than he normally did, but she'd never known Bart to lose control. He had to have ruined the perfect illusion Olivia had created of their life on purpose. But for what reason? The only thing she could think of was that she'd defied him by leaving their table. Bart didn't do well with defiance, especially from his wife, and this was a punishment. But did he understand what this would do? This wasn't just some petty attempt at revenge. This would change their lives. Did he know that now Olivia had to make a life-altering decision?

Could she stay even while her whole world knew what she was enduring on a daily basis? That she was living with a man who didn't love her, who may have never loved her. Olivia once again pushed back at the tears that came to her eyes. She was pretty sure she knew what she had to do but dreaded it. Olivia had hoped to shelter her daughters from the discord in her marriage and life, but now it wouldn't be possible. She was sure the news of the real reason Bart didn't live on the island would be spreading like wildfire.

"How about pancakes for breakfast?" Olivia asked, pushing all turmoil from the forefront of her mind, and both of her girls froze.

"Real pancakes?" Rachel asked when she came out of her stupor. Bart was a big proponent of whole foods, keeping processed foods out of their mouths and their home. Even when he wasn't around, he made sure Patty knew his stance on the matter to ensure that Olivia followed his regimented diet along with the girls.

But Olivia wasn't feeling much like following her husband at the moment. Especially when she remembered that she'd asked Patty to grab a pancake mix for Olivia to use as a base for the quiche she'd made for one of her elderly neighbors the week before—he loved a comforting quiche something fierce. And that box of mix sat on her pantry shelf, three-quarters full. The idea of not having to use almond flour as a substitute for the refined stuff Bart hated so much made Olivia genuinely smile.

"With lots of fruit as a topping," Olivia said, mostly because she knew there wouldn't be syrup of any kind in their kitchen. The pancake mix had been a one-time miracle in the Birmingham home, and pancakes needed a sweet topper.

"Yes!" Pearl yelled, and both girls scrambled off of Olivia's light purple duvet and toward the back staircase that would send them directly to the kitchen.

Olivia followed behind her girls, smiling her first genuine smile since the night before. She liked to think that she had endured her life for the sake of her daughters. They deserved the lifestyle Bart's hard work gave them and a world where their mother and father were a unit. Granted, Olivia couldn't remember the last time she'd felt at one with Bart.

The first few years after she'd found out about the affairs had been miserable. Olivia had been sure she'd leave at any moment. But for some reason she couldn't now remember, she had stayed. And then she'd gotten pregnant with Rachel, and the idea of doing it all on her own seemed impossible. So she'd once again stayed. Not that she didn't think about leaving Bart every day. She did. But courage wasn't Olivia's strong suit, and the fear of everyone knowing that Bart was cheating on her and the fear of the unknown were overwhelming. The pain she lived through every day had become a constant companion; she knew how to deal with that. But she also knew a whole different pain would come with leaving, one she wasn't sure she could bear. But now that everyone knew about Bart's cheating, she wondered if this was finally the time to walk away?

She watched as her girls laughed and pulled out bowls and pans, comfortable with their surroundings. Comfortable in the only home they'd ever known. Could Olivia take that away from them? Because she knew in her heart there was no way she'd stay in that house if she separated from Bart.

Even though Olivia had left her mark on every inch of the five thousand square feet, she knew this space did and would always belong to Bart. This was his house. His name was the only one on the deed and the mortgage. It was part of why Olivia had been so adamant about decorating the space. She'd hoped that would help her to feel more like this was also her home. And maybe it kind of had, but not enough for her to think that she could possibly wrestle the home away from Bart in a divorce settlement. He'd never let that happen, and honestly, it wasn't worth the battle.

The way divorce settlement rolled so easily through her mind startled Olivia. Was that the next step?

She absentmindedly put the pancake mix, eggs, and milk onto the counter before mixing them together and pouring them into the pan to cook. Her girls had oohed and ahhed over the process, but Olivia couldn't slow her thoughts.

Of course divorce was the next step if she was going to leave Bart. She couldn't move out of his home and then expect to keep his ring on her finger. Besides, did the significance of that ring even matter anymore? What did marriage even mean to Bart?

She'd been faithful to him in every form of the word. She'd never even looked at another man that way—more because that was what she expected from marriage, and she had to be true to her own beliefs, even if Bart didn't respect her and their vows in the same way—and she'd done exactly what Bart expected of his wife. And what had she gotten in return? She was sure in Bart's mind that the beautiful home, the limitless credit cards, and access to his lifestyle were more than enough of a return for anything Olivia could possibly give him.

But should she stay? Deep down she knew severing ties with Bart would mean the same for the girls. Bart had never been an involved father. He loved the girls in his own way, but his life was too busy for children; he'd always said as much. When Olivia had told Bart about her first pregnancy, she'd hoped that could change things. But it had ended up being one of the worst hurts of all. He'd left that night to go to his mistresses, claiming that he needed time to wrap his mind around the fact that Olivia was pregnant.

He'd come home the next weekend all smiles, but that first reaction of his had nearly killed Olivia's spirit. And so, she'd packed her bags while he'd been away, but his coming back had been enough for Olivia to unpack and stay for the umpteenth time in her marriage.

Would she finally have the courage to walk away now?

"Pancakes are up," Olivia said with the fake cheer she'd mastered over the years. She passed a plate to each of her beaming girls and then eyed the batter. Should she make herself a batch? Bart was constantly on her to lose a few more pounds. He hated when she wasn't in, what he liked to call, top form.

Defiance filling her for the second time in as many days, Olivia poured the batter for own batch, going so far as to get the butter out of the fridge to lather up her pancakes after she put some on her girls' stacks.

The girls happily took their plates to the breakfast bar as they debated over what kind of fruit to top their treat with, and something hit Olivia hard. They'd been up and together for nearly an hour now, and not once had her daughters asked about their father. They knew he was at home because Olivia had told them he was going to the reunion the night before. But even though they hadn't seen him in two weeks, neither girl did what Olivia would have done as a child if her father had been away: run into his room and get him up the way her girls had done with her. If her mother had for some reason kept Olivia away from her dad, Olivia would've been chomping at the bit, asking her mother every two seconds when dad would be joining them for breakfast. But as Rachel and Pearl chattered away between bites of pancakes, neither even looked toward the kitchen entry to see if their father would be joining them. Was this Olivia's answer?

"Pancakes. Really, Olivia?" Bart's deep voice entered the kitchen before he did, and both Pearl and Rachel gave Olivia a worried look before turning back to their half empty plates. The man had always had a nose like a hound.

Olivia didn't say anything as she defiantly looked at the entryway Bart was about to enter through. She heard the door to the bathroom off the kitchen open and then close, giving them a bit more time. Olivia realized she should take this moment to clear her daughters out of the room. She and Bart needed to talk about things that sweet little ears didn't need to hear.

"Girls, why don't you take those plates up to your room and finish your breakfast up there?" Olivia offered, and both girls smiled at their mother before scrambling out of their chairs, nearly running with their plates up the back staircase. They both knew their pancakes could be in jeopardy if their dad got a hold of them.

Olivia flipped her own pancakes onto her plate and

proceeded to cut a banana to top them as Bart entered the kitchen. He was, unsurprisingly, ready for the day. His hair was slicked back, and he was already dressed in a pair of khakis and a blue polo shirt, Bart's typical weekend gear.

"I guess this means you're moving out," Bart said as he walked to the cabinet and took out a glass before filling it with water from the pitcher in the fridge.

Olivia dropped her butter knife she'd been using to cut the banana and let it clatter to the counter, startled by Bart's words. That had not been what she'd been expecting.

"I saw your face last night, Olivia, and now pancakes for you and the girls this morning?"

Bart held the cold glass to his forehead for a second, reminding Olivia that her husband was probably suffering from a pretty massive hangover. When he suddenly moved to go to the cabinet where they kept their ibuprofen, she knew that was the case.

"Pancakes mean I'm leaving you?" Olivia asked, and Bart threw back his pills before downing the rest of his water.

"It's been a long time coming," Bart said, adding, "Let's not draw this out. I know you're planning on going to your parents. I can send all of the paperwork there."

Olivia stared in shock at the man she'd been tied to for nearly half of her life, more than half if she counted the years they'd dated. How could he be so nonchalant about this all? It was tearing her up inside to even think about leaving Bart, and this was his reaction? She knew he didn't care as much as she did, but did he care at all?

"I want this to be as amicable as possible. I'll be generous in my child support as well as spousal support," Bart said, as if that was what Olivia cared about. But it always came down to money with Bart.

"I texted Lenny last night. He'll get this thing going," Bart continued when Olivia said nothing. Olivia registered that Bart had mentioned the name of his lawyer and that he'd texted him last night. Bart was doing it again. This should have been Olivia's moment to decide what she wanted to do with the rest of her life, but like everything else, Bart had taken over. Why was she surprised? This was her life.

Olivia swallowed before saying, "Did you consider that I would want to try to work this out?" She was hoping to startle her husband a fraction of the amount he'd shaken her.

"Do you?" he asked, seeming unfazed in the least.

"I don't know," Olivia said as she pulled her robe tighter to her body. Most mornings Bart was home, she would have been fully dressed and made up long before Bart woke up. But again, this morning was different. Maybe this was what Bart saw? This was why he knew it was over? Had she given her opinion on the matter so loudly with her actions that she didn't need to say a word? But he should have given her the chance to say them. And he'd texted Lenny last night.

"How can you be so calm about this? Our entire lives are changing," Olivia said. Then she realized that wasn't really the case. She and the girls would be moving. She and the girls would be changing their lifestyles. She and the girls would deal with the gossip on Whisling. Nothing would change for Bart other than that they wouldn't be here to greet him on the weekends. Weekends where he spent most of his time without them anyway.

Tears began to fall down Olivia's cheeks. She willed herself to be angry. Anger would be the far better emotion. But Olivia was so sad, nothing else could find a way through. She'd swallowed everything for so long, and this was where it had gotten her? Who could she blame other than herself?

"Please don't make a scene, Olivia," Bart said, and Oliva wanted to scoff. Bart had always been just as worried about appearances as Olivia—another reason why she couldn't believe he'd let the truth come out—but who was here to see her if she broke down? She then realized he was only protecting himself. Bart didn't want to witness her scene. Well, too bad for him.

Olivia let out a sob and another quickly followed. They were unable to be kept in now that she'd let loose on her control of her body and emotions.

"Olivia," Bart admonished. He stood and walked toward the windows on the other side of the kitchen, as far away from Olivia as he could get.

Olivia rubbed at her makeupless eyes, suddenly hating that she was letting Bart see her lose it. She didn't want him to know how much he'd hurt her. How much she hated that this was their end. Especially when she'd seen him much more impassioned and emotional over business deals than he was about their marriage being over. He didn't deserve her sorrow. And yet, she felt it deeply.

She stood tall, sensing something bubble up within her that felt foreign. But she liked whatever it was because it gave her the voice to say what she needed to next.

"You're right. I'm leaving." Olivia said the words and was proud of herself for her decision, even if it was fifteen years too late. Her daughters deserved more. She'd never seen it so clearly as she did that moment.

Bart turned around and nodded, the glazed look in his eyes telling her he was already bored of the conversation. He'd written her out of his heart years ago, so it made writing her out of his life easy. She wished she'd done the same, but she'd never been able to get her whole heart back from Bart. Even after all of the cheating and all of the neglect, she still loved him. But she shook off those feelings to, for once, stand up for her daughters. Why had it taken her so long to do so? However, now wasn't the time to beat herself up about that. There'd be plenty of time for that later.

"But I'd like you to leave the house so that I can tell our girls the news in my way. That is nonnegotiable," Olivia said, standing firm on the one thing she cared about. She nearly felt a spark of joy through her sadness at the shock on Bart's face. Finally.

Bart walked out of the kitchen without saying another word. She knew he'd hate that she'd put her foot down about anything, but his walking out without an argument told her that he didn't find their girls worth fighting for, which added a whole new dimension to Olivia's pain. Olivia listened as his footsteps faded away from the kitchen, and then she saw his red Aston Martin tear down the driveway.

And this was their end.

SIX

BESS WASN'T SURPRISED when she heard her front door open and close, followed by the clicking of Deb's heeled boots against her hardwood floors. She'd known it wouldn't be long after the local news aired that her best friend would show up.

Bess wasn't sure she wanted Deb here yet. She was still processing this additional burden to be dropped on her already heavy heart. Word of her husband's affair had suddenly become a news story.

Earlier that morning, Jon had tried to call. Bess had ignored that call, the same way she had all of his other calls during the past four weeks, but then a text had come. Bess was too curious to ignore that; Jon hated texting.

His words had knocked her world off its axis, not that it was all that well aligned after the recent events of her life anyway. She'd spent every day of the last four weeks alternating between extreme sadness and anger, and then just trying to pick herself back up.

In his text, Jon had explained that after his one indiscretion —he was still sticking to that story—Jon had reassigned his aide to another professor. The aide was furious, and for some reason, four weeks after the whole mess first started, she sought retribution by going to the school newspaper.

Evidently, it was a slow news cycle or the local news needed a juicy tabloidesque tidbit of information because now everyone was running with the story that a married professor had had an affair with his teacher's aide, then fired her to hide it. Jon, and now his lawyer, were insisting the aide was reassigned to a position with the same pay and same hours, nowhere near being fired. But the damage had been done, and even the university was trying to figure out what to do. On top of everything, Jon might lose his job.

Jon went on to text how sorry he was. But Bess was sick of it. Of course he was sorry. He was ruining his life.

Bess would have never claimed their marriage was perfect at any time in their lives, even more so recently. There had been a slow growing rift between Jon and herself in the years since they'd become empty nesters, and neither of them had made it a priority to mend that rift.

When the kids had been young, it had been their number one priority to work on their marriage. Weekly dates, getting the kids to bed on time so that they could talk and enjoy one another, even couples' vacations. But when their baby, James, moved out, it became so easy to spend time together that they got lazy with it. Date nights stopped, and their conversations were no longer a priority. Television became their nightly routine, and they lost part of their connection. But Bess had never thought it would come to this. How had it come to this? She thought about texting Jon her question. She knew he would try to answer her. But she didn't.

Bess had been sitting on her couch just staring out at the dark blue surf hitting the cream colored sand of the cove beyond her window for the last two hours since she'd gotten the news, processing. And maybe doing a little bit of investigative work into the atrocious news story.

"Please tell me the Jon Wilder all over the news isn't your Jon Wilder?" Deb said as she came into Bess' living room, this time with no food from the kitchen in her hands which meant circumstances were dire. Especially since Bess had a whole plate of brownies just sitting on the counter.

"You mean the professor whose picture looks exactly like my husband?" Bess asked, and she suddenly felt the urge to laugh. The situation her life was in was so far from comical, it almost came back around to being funny. Almost.

"Bess." Deb joined Bess on her big brown couch and pulled her friend into a hug.

Bess fell into Deb's arms, needing their comfort even though she still wasn't really ready to talk. But ready or not, Deb was here, and Bess knew in the end it would be for the best. Deb pushed her, and for that she was almost always grateful.

"It's really not too much worse than before," Bess said from within Deb's embrace.

Deb pulled back to look Bess in the eye. "It's not?" Deb asked, her face telling Bess she thought it was.

"Sure, now everyone knows my business, but it wasn't like I thought it could stay a secret forever. And at least I already told the kids weeks ago. Even though I worry how this being public will affect them. Fortunately, since James decided to go to UDub instead of Jon's school, hopefully the backlash won't bother the kids."

"But won't it bother you?" Deb asked.

Bess shrugged as she pulled all the way out of Deb's hug. "I guess it will. But people are going to talk. My children and my friends are whose opinions I care about, and all of you are on my side. It doesn't matter what the news says."

"That's right," Deb said fervently, ever the loyal friend.

"Besides, I think that part will all blow over soon. And as far as Jon's job, that's more about him. We've been smart about saving over the years, and we can live comfortably on what we have for a long time."

"We. So does that mean you aren't leaving him?" Deb asked, prying a little too deep for Bess' liking, especially because Bess knew Deb's opinion on that. She believed Bess should already be long gone.

"He's not here, is he?" Bess asked, and Deb shook her head.

"That's the only answer I've got for now," Bess said.

Deb nodded, unnaturally unopinionated. "So you saw the story?" Deb asked.

Bess nodded. She'd debated whether to look it up online after Jon had warned her about it and she, in turn, had warned her kids. They'd all texted back various forms of "I'll be fine," but they were worried for her. She insisted she would be fine as well. And considering how terrible this should be, she was. The real blow had been when Jon had told her about the affair. That part still tore at her gut. But this? The humiliation was real, there was no doubt about that, but the pain of humiliation wasn't anything like that first pain.

So against her better judgement, Bess had decided to dig more and easily found the story. Pictures of Jon and his aide were everywhere. And she was beautiful.

That hadn't shocked Bess, but it wasn't exactly an ego boost either. She had kind of hoped ... what had she hoped? Was there room for hope in a situation like this one?

Bess vowed to herself that after that first investigatory dig, no more. She wanted no more details, no more information. If she was ever going to forgive Jon, she needed to move on. And that meant not reliving every sordid detail by rereading or rehearing the accounts.

Even if she *wasn't* going to forgive Jon, she needed to move on. For her own good, she was putting it all behind her. Others could talk, but she speculated they wouldn't for long. Most of the people on the island were good people, the kind who didn't revel in the downfall of others. Not all, but she'd just avoid that contingent for the time being.

Bess needed to look to her future, whatever that was.

She thought about Deb's question. Was she going to take Jon back? *That* she didn't know. But it was a question she was okay with having unanswered for the time being.

However, that didn't mean her life could be on hold. She had to figure out what she wanted to do now. Not she and Jon, not she and her children, but Bess. Just Bess.

Because her past was hyper-focused on her family didn't mean her future had to be as well. Of course she'd still keep her children at the forefront of her life, but they were off on their own and away from the island for now, giving Bess a whole lot of free time. So what was she going to do with it? She figured finding a way to fill that time, maybe with a job, was her number one priority. She'd been fine with filling her days with nothing for a while, but now that was exhausting her. It seemed silly that she'd once been exhausted by looking to the future, and now just living felt exhausting. But the emotions raging through her at all times made this unexpected phase of life unpredictable and unlike any other. Bess had learned to just go with what she felt. And right now she felt the need to find some purpose in her life. ASAP.

"But I don't want to see the story again," Bess said, allowing her rapidly running thoughts to pause long enough to go back to her conversation with Deb.

"You're moving on," Deb said, completely understanding what Bess wanted and needed with just those few words.

A relationship like the one she had with Deb was one of a kind. Deb might push and dig past the point of comfort, but she was always just what Bess needed. Their friendship was built on years and years of communication, love, and even fights, and they always came out stronger in the end.

"From the story and Jon's indiscretion," Bess reiterated, and Deb nodded.

"I need to clear that out of my mind so I can focus on my future," Bess said, and Deb nodded again.

"You are so strong, Bess," Deb said with tears in her eyes.

But Bess couldn't agree. She didn't feel close to being strong. She was just surviving. So Bess ignored that and pulled out her notepad that she kept in the side table next to the couch. She loved to jot down her thoughts when she could, but the book was mostly filled with tasks that needed to be completed later and shopping lists.

This was going to be different.

Bess opened to a blank page and wrote along the top: Occupations.

"Good, great," Deb said as she read over Bess' shoulder.

Bess tapped her pen against the paper. It had been a grand gesture, but now what to do?

"Teacher," Deb offered, and Bess wrote it down, even though it wasn't truly an option in her mind. But she had to start with something.

"I thought you loved teaching." Deb said when she noticed Bess' face.

"I did. But the thought of going back to continuing education classes and then having to keep up with hormonal teenagers?" Bess said.

Deb laughed. "I can see your point," she said and then went back to staring at the nearly nonexistent list along with Bess.

"Who's going to hire a woman my age with nearly no work experience?" Bess asked, suddenly feeling like this task might be too great. Why hadn't she insisted on working once her kids were back in school? She knew why. She loved being at home with them and wouldn't have traded that time for the world, even knowing her present situation. But that love didn't help her in this particular moment.

"You managed a home and family for over twenty years. That has to count for something," Deb said.

Bess raised an eyebrow at her friend. "It meant something to the kids...." Bess' voice trailed off because she was going to say, "And Jon." But that statement no longer felt right, and she hated that. "But not to the rest of the world."

Deb pursed her lips and then said, "Well, finding a job is all about who you know these days anyway."

Bess looked around the empty room and then back at Deb. "I know you," Bess said.

"I'm sure I could put some feelers out at the art studios and ..." Deb began before Bess cut her off.

"That wasn't what I was meaning. I don't want you to find me a job. Besides, I'd probably go crazy with too many of you artsy types," Bess said with a grin, and Deb laughed.

Bess heard her front door open and close again before Gen ran into the room.

"The gossip is already running rampant at the salon?" Bess asked.

Gen just sat on the couch beside her sister.

"I'm okay, Gen," Bess said as her sister gathered her into a hug. It occurred to Bess that maybe her sister wasn't okay, so she more than readily returned her sister's hug.

"I had to finish Mrs. Donnelly's cut, but I cancelled the rest of my day," Gen said.

Bess held her sister a little tighter. She didn't know what she would have done without her family and Deb.

"You didn't need to do that," Bess said.

Gen nodded against her shoulder. "You've always been the

strong one. But I did need to do this. Maybe for both of us," she said, practically admitting how hard the news had hit her.

"What are you doing?" Gen asked as she finally let go of Bess and turned to the notepad that sat open on the coffee table.

"Your sister needs a job," Deb said, and Bess nodded.

"If this is about money, Levi and I would be happy to—" Gen stopped speaking as Bess shook her head. She and her sister hardly ever talked finances, so she didn't know that Bess and Jon were more than okay in that aspect. At least one part of her life hadn't gone to the dogs.

"I need something to occupy my time," Bess said honestly. She'd spent the last month cooking way too much food but couldn't keep that up forever. Her neighbors were still loving all of the extra meals, but how long would that last?

"Got it," Gen said as she looked at Bess and then back at the list. "What about my salon? I could always use a receptionist. Or I'm sure Levi could use your management skills at his company. Last I heard, his most recent scheduling guy had him in two places at the same time. Levi had to turn the charm way up to get them out of that one," Gen said.

Bess shook her head. She loved her family, but she couldn't work for them. "It's just ..." Bess began.

Gen smiled. "I get it," she responded with a small smile before standing, seeming a lot better than she had been when she'd walked into Bess' home. Having a purpose like finding Bess a job was good for all three of them. "I think this conversation calls for something sweet. Have you still been baking, Bess?" Gen asked, and Bess nodded.

"There are brownies, frosted sugar cookies, and dulce de leche cake," Bess said.

Deb's eyes went wide in awe, and Gen grinned before getting up to get a snack.

"Grab me a brownie," Deb said to Gen's retreating back from her spot on the couch.

"Bess, this is so much food!" Gen said from the kitchen before coming out with a piece of cake and Deb's brownie.

Bess knew her fridge and freezer were stuffed with leftovers from her creations. But again, she'd had a lot of time and only so many neighbors.

Gen gave Deb her brownie, who immediately inhaled the baked good, before sitting back on the other side of Bess.

"Oh my word," Gen moaned as she swallowed a bite of cake. "I swear this is the best thing I've eaten since the last time you fed me," Gen said, and Bess chuckled.

"It's not a joke, Bess," Gen said as she put another bite into her mouth.

Deb nodded in agreement. "Your food is much better than any restaurant on the island. Heck, it's better than any fare I've tasted anywhere," Deb said. But Bess didn't believe her friend. The woman had literally traveled the whole world as a flight attendant and had eaten at some of the best food establishments the planet had to offer.

"I've got it!" Gen said as she up straight and turned to Bess and then Deb with excitement all over her face.

"Nope." Bess immediately vetoed Gen's idea.

"But I didn't even say anything yet." Gen's eyes went wide at her sister's declaration. It wasn't like Bess to not even hear what she had to say.

"Your left eye is doing that twitch. It means the idea is whacky. I've got enough whacky in my life for the time being," Bess said, and Deb nodded from where she sat on the other side of the couch but then stopped suddenly.

"I agree that you are dealing with lots of whacky, but I vote we hear Gen out. Maybe her kind of whacky is exactly what you need?" Deb said.

Bess looked from her best friend to her sister. She liked things neat and orderly. Her life had always been that way because she was a planner. They'd once taken a cross country road trip with all of their children, and Bess had been the one to prepare for it. She meticulously went through the road map, finding places for possible potty breaks every twenty miles. And when that wasn't possible, she came up with contingency plans. They had reservations at hotels months in advance, and then contingencies for if they couldn't make it to the appointed hotel on time each night. The trip had been a blast for everyone involved, but she remembered that Jon had looked over at her one night as she poured over plans for the next day and said in a kind tone, "Maybe it would be fun to leave something to chance." Bess laughed, sure that it was a joke, and Jon laughed along with her. But now she wondered if Jon had meant what he'd said. Did he want less of a plan in his life? Was that why he'd blown Bess' carefully laid future to smithereens? An affair wasn't on Bess' life roadmap, that was for sure.

"Maybe I could convince the food panty or the library to make my volunteer positions full-time, paid positions," Bess said, trying to find an idea that didn't involve whacky. Her savings might be giving her a good cushion for the time being, but that didn't mean she never had to bring in an income again. Her volunteer positions provided moral satisfaction, but you couldn't live on that. Now that she was looking at the possibility of being on her own, she should probably think of a way to add to her savings instead of just pulling from them indefinitely.

"My idea is better," Gen said at the same time Deb asked, "Is that even possible?"

Volunteer work had been Bess' initial plan for the years after her children moved out. She'd always been closely associated with the food pantry, and after her children all left home, she started volunteering there much more frequently. But she found that she still had too much free time, so she decided to go to the public library on the island and offered her services to them. At the moment, she went in a few days a week and re-shelved books. She didn't have a set schedule, per say; she just went in whenever she could. But she thought about how understaffed the place was. Deb was right. Bess was pretty sure, even without asking, that there wasn't enough money in the library budget to take her on as an actual employee.

The food pantry was a little bit different because she'd volunteered there for so long. Maybe she could become an employee if she really needed the money. She knew other volunteers had moved up the ranks to paid positions over time. But the few paid positions were typically just part-time; could Bess live on a part-time income for the rest of her life? With her savings, maybe, but who knew when the next paid position at the food bank would open?

Bess sank back into the couch as she realized she agreed with her best friend. Her suggestion wasn't possible. So where did that leave her?

"Are you ready to hear me out?" Gen said.

Bess reluctantly turned to her sister. It was just an idea. One Bess could easily veto if she hated it. But hating the idea wasn't what scared Bess. Gen knew her, and Bess was scared that the idea Gen had would be exactly what Bess needed but totally out of her comfort zone.

But wasn't everything she was going through out of her comfort zone? And on the plus side, she'd hardly had any time to think about the whole Jon situation since the conversation had turned to her future. She'd count that as a win for the day.

Bess was pretty sure she'd have a breakdown later that night in the safety of her bed, when other thoughts gave way to the lack of her husband beside her. But every moment she could continue to live and push forward in life was positive for Bess, and she needed that. She was done with wasting all of her days and nights mourning what could have been. What should have been.

Bess raised an eyebrow instead of answering, but Gen got the message and began to speak. "Your food is incredible," Gen began, and Bess turned to Deb to see her nodding at Gen's declaration. But this wasn't anything new. Her sister and best friend had always pumped her up about her food.

"You love to cook and bake," Gen said, so Bess turned her attention back to her sister.

That was true. It had been one of her saving graces through all of this. It had softened the blow when she'd told her children about the fact that their father was no longer living in their childhood home, it had occupied her mind when she'd needed to just get away from it all, and although it wasn't good for her waistline, it had also been delicious, a bright spot when she'd needed it.

"So why not do that?" Gen asked, looking at Bess expectantly.

"Do what?" Bess asked. So far she saw no plan for a future in what Gen was saying.

"Cook," Gen said.

Bess shook her head. That would never work. "I have no formal training. The restaurants here on the island, at least the nicer ones where I'd want to work, are all run by professional chefs. I doubt they'd even want me in their kitchens peeling their potatoes," Bess said, sorry to shut down Gen's idea immediately. But Bess had actually already had a fleeting thought in the same direction. She'd wondered what if, just because she did love to cook so much. But it wasn't possible.

"Then start your own restaurant," Deb said as she stood and scooted around Bess so that she could sit on the coffee table and

be a part of the conversation instead of blocked because she was
sitting behind Bess.

"The statistics on that are terrible," Bess said as she shook
her head. Sure, she had some money to invest in herself. But
that was too risky. The overhead of a brick and mortar store was
astronomical, especially on the island.

Deb pursed her lips as she thought, but it was Gen who
spoke. "Last time I was in Seattle, I realized something on the
ferry home."

Bess cocked her head as she listened to her sister.

"The food scene in Seattle is booming," Gen said.

That was the truth. She and Jon had often gone on dates
into the city just to taste some of the new cuisines the place had
to offer.

"Not like here at all," Bess said, and Gen nodded. Did her
sister think she should start a venture in Seattle? That wasn't
going to happen. She imagined the hours it took to start a restaurant and doubted that would allow her to come home very often.
Not only would she have to front the money for an entire new
restaurant, she'd probably have to find a place to stay while she
did it. The costs would add up fast, and her savings would evap-
orate in no time. If the restaurant wasn't an immediate success ...
it was just too risky.

"And we're missing that here," Gen said.

Bess realized they were back to this, building the new business on Whisling. But had Gen seen rent for even the smallest
of spaces on the island? Well, she had since she had her own
business in the heart of town, but did she know how much Bess
would have to make back in order to pay for that small space?
A lot.

"That's true. Sometimes I am craving a good home-cooked
meal like the ones you serve, but all we have are our swanky
seafood places or the grease pits." Deb used the nickname she

had for anything fast food. She actually said the name affection-
ately because Deb quite often frequented those grease pits, but
Bess understood what she meant.

There were quite a few nights while she had been raising
her children when Bess would've loved to have someone else
make her a pasta dish for a reasonable price. The girls were
right; the island didn't have a place like that. But it was probably
for the same reasons Bess couldn't start one. It was too expensive
on the island to sell quality food at decent prices. After paying
rent and then shipping the food, costs would have to be bumped
up significantly.

"But rent would kill me," Bess said.

Gen nodded like she'd been ready for that argument. "A
food truck," she said.

Bess leaned back into the couch as if she'd been hit by Gen's
words. Gen couldn't be serious.

"A food truck," Deb said slowly as if she were trying the idea
on for size. But the idea wouldn't fit. Because it was crazy.

"That's ridiculous," Bess said. But even as she said it, a tiny
doubt niggled at her mind. Was it ridiculous? Or was it genius?
This was why she had been fearful about what Gen was going
to say. She knew it would be tempting. And the more Bess
thought about a food truck, the more tempting it became.
Owning her own business instead of working for someone else
was the dream. Creating her own menu, seeing people eat and
enjoy her food every day. And the food truck would be much
less of an overhead cost than an actual storefront. But the cost of
food would still be outrageous, right?

"I can see those wheels turning, so let me help them along,"
Gen said. "Levi has a friend who started a food truck on one of
the San Juan islands."

Bess stared at her sister, waiting as the information came in.
The San Juan islands were north of Whisling and were even

more secluded. At least Whisling, which sat right in the middle of the Puget Sound with a ferry that came directly from Seattle, was more accessible than the San Juan Islands which had to use the ferry from Anacortes.

"And he's doing really well. I'm sure I could get you in contact with him. Levi also has a friend who works at Labor and Industries, and I'm sure he would be happy to help you get things started."

It didn't surprise Bess that her brother-in-law had connections everywhere. He was a social guy, and everyone loved him. But a food truck? Really?

Bess recalled eating at a taco truck with Stephen when she'd taken him to school, and she'd seen her handsome son's face alight with delight as he dove into the fare while seated at a plastic table on the side of the road. It wasn't a place Bess would have frequented, but she understood the appeal as a patron. Now, trying to see it from a vendor's point of view, she had to admit it was attractive. The cost of the truck up front would be big, but after that she'd own it. And she could always sell it again if times got too hard.

"I can talk to Noel at the Landing." Deb mentioned the highly acclaimed seafood restaurant that had tourists coming in droves to Whisling. "I'm sure he's got an idea of how much it would cost you to bring in your supplies."

"You're friends with the head chef at the Landing?" Bess asked, and Deb shrugged.

"They acquired a few of my paintings, and Noel sought me out when we ate there a few months back. He comped my meal, and we've been on friendly terms ever since."

Bess smiled, unsurprised at the gesture. Deb's paintings were incredible and often had people fawning over her, becoming immediate fans of her work.

"So what do you think?" Gen asked.

Bess stood and walked to the kitchen, needing to do more than just sit on the couch to make such a big decision.

She pulled out a tray of meatballs from the fridge that she'd already formed earlier that afternoon and then a frying pan. She poured in some oil, let it get hot, and then dropped the meatballs in.

Gen and Deb followed her, sitting at the barstools at her kitchen island while they gave her time and watched her work.

"This is a big deal," Bess said, and Gen nodded.

"Huge," Deb agreed.

"If I fail, it would also be big," Bess said.

"It would," Gen said. Then she added, "But I don't think you'll fail. Your food is fantastic."

"If all it took was good food to be successful, chefs wouldn't need to cook at restaurants owned by businessmen," Bess said.

Gen nodded once. She had to agree with that.

"But you have business savvy people on your side, Bess," Gen said, and Deb nodded. The two women who sat beside her had both started their own businesses. Levi owned the island's best construction company, and his food truck friend would also be a great resource.

However, Bess had never been great with numbers. Sure, she kept track of their family finances, but when it came to doing their taxes each year, which she also did herself, she hated it. She often prayed when she sent in her return that she'd done everything right. She knew she did them to the best of her ability, but those few weeks every year were some of her worst.

However, it would be thrilling to serve her food to strangers and have them pay her in return.

That thrill overrode her fears, and Bess began to see the puzzle pieces fall into place. She could find someone to help her with the books when they became too much, but at first she was sure she could handle them. She might hate that part, but her joy of cooking would be so full, would anything be able to get her down? She was quite certain she had more than enough in her savings to buy what she needed. She'd have to talk to Levi's friends and crunch lots and lots of numbers, write up a business plan, and find a food truck. The tasks began to overwhelm her. Could she do this?

The more important question. Did she want to do this? As the aroma of her meatballs hit her nose and she watched each one turn perfectly brown, she knew her answer to that. It was a resounding yes. There was nothing she wanted to do more with her life.

Bess had never been one to go out on a limb for a want of her own. Of course she did it for the needs of her family and even their wants. But for herself?

"You can do this, Bess," Deb said with a confidence that was contagious.

She could, right? She could at least try. She had to at least try.

"Let's open a food truck," Bess said.

SEVEN

OLIVIA LOOKED AROUND at her new space that had once been her childhood bedroom. In the month and a half since she'd been home, she'd spruced it up a bit by taking down posters of her teenaged obsessions and adding pictures of her daughters to the white walls. Her twin bed was now a queen, which her girls often found their way into in the middle of the night, even though Olivia and her parents had converted their guest room into a pink haven for Rachel and Pearl. But this move had been hard on her girls, especially Pearl. They often asked for Patty, but what broke Olivia's heart the most was that they didn't ask for their father. They knew the man had had little time for them before. It was as if they sensed he was even less interested in them now. Her dad did his best to make their new home full of his presence and fun, but that couldn't be enough. A girl needed her dad, didn't she? Olivia knew *she* did. But that was something she'd neglected to give her daughters, and for that she wasn't sure she could ever forgive herself.

Her parents had been more than happy to let her come home. Maybe even a little thrilled. They were devastated for

Olivia because they knew that she felt terrible about the demise of her life as she knew it, but they'd been kindly telling her for years that something had to change. She knew that they'd seen how miserable she was but felt there was little they could do about it when Olivia wouldn't even acknowledge that there was a problem. Her mother had even gone so far as to tell Olivia her home was open to her and her children any time, no questions asked. So now Olivia was taking them up on that. And so much more. After her initial anger had subsided, which lasted all of a few days, Olivia had been little more than a shell of her former self. Her parents had been there for her girls when Olivia just couldn't.

Now, the days were feeling a little less long and dark. Olivia's sweet girls had helped to begin her healing process. She just hoped she was doing as much for them.

So here she was. Now what?

She didn't want to focus on her divorce. Thankfully, Bart's attorney would be taking care of all of that. Her brother had recommended an attorney, and her parents had been all for the guy, but Olivia told them she had it taken care of. Her family didn't push. They knew she was incredibly fragile, and they were being extremely sensitive to that.

Although Olivia had wondered for a minute if she should have her own attorney, she'd decided to let Lenny get the job done quickly. After all, who would better represent her during this divorce than Lenny, a friend since college. Sure, he'd become Bart's personal attorney in the subsequent years, but she'd introduced Lenny to his wife, Ana, for heaven's sake. They were practically family. Besides, the last thing she wanted to do was deal with any of this mess on her own.

However, if she were going to take an attorney recommendation from anyone, it would be from her brother. There was no man Olivia trusted more than her brother, Dax. He was a few years her senior and now lived in Nashville, managing the career of country superstar, Ellis Rider. Even with his busy life, he'd offered to fly home the minute he'd heard the news. When Olivia had told him to stay where he was needed in Nashville, he'd made her promise she'd reach out if she needed anything.

Although her initial anger was gone and her empty shell was beginning to feel a little more alive again, Olivia still felt tired. So tired. Especially when her girls weren't around.

Olivia made her way to the kitchen. Her parents' home was much like most of the others on the island. It sat on one of the secluded coves on the west side of the island. The four-bedroom beach bungalow had been a perfect place to grow up, but Olivia had to wonder what her daughters thought of it now after living in Bart's home all of their lives. Her parents' home was a one-story with an open floor plan where the homey kitchen was only separated from the living room by a reclaimed driftwood island counter and barstools, unlike the secluded and enormous kitchen in Bart's house which had been divided from the rest of the home, the domain clearly marked for Patty. Her parents' couches were a blue gray that matched the ocean just beyond their windows and were worn and well loved. The couches Olivia had chosen for Bart's home still looked brand new, even though two children resided there, because Bart demanded they be traded out every year or so. He had only entertained clients at their Whisling home twice, but he'd always wanted their home to be up to par just in case. Olivia had been happy to keep up appearances of perfection in every way.

But now that that perfect bubble had been shattered, Olivia didn't know what to do. There was no faking it anymore. Part of her felt immense relief, while the other part felt like she was missing the piece that had kept things together for so long. And without it, would she fall apart? Was she already falling apart?

Barefooted, Olivia stepped into the kitchen that was just a

few yards from her bedroom—very unlike the trek she had to take to get breakfast in Bart's house. She'd already seen the girls off to school and should have eaten her first meal of the day along with them, but she didn't have it in her to do so. Eating was a chore she didn't feel up to most days, but she knew if she skipped one more meal, her mother wouldn't be happy. When she'd taken Olivia into a hug when Olivia had first moved home, the first thing her mom had said after comforting her was that she needed to eat. So Olivia had been doing her best to get something into her system three times a day. But her clothes were still fitting too loosely, and she knew she was going to have to step it up. Maybe today would be that day?

Olivia thought about cereal, oatmeal, toast, eggs, but none of it sounded appealing. Fortunately, the cooking skills her mom had instilled in her as a teenager hadn't disappeared with lack of use, even though Patty had taken care of feeding them almost every day for the last fifteen years. But although Olivia could cook, she didn't want to.

She stuck her head into the white refrigerator that wore dozens of magnets from her parents travels, hoping for a miracle that she'd see something she wanted to eat. She smiled an actual genuine smile when she saw a plate of cheesy pasta covered with cling film. She could do cheesy pasta.

Olivia took out a plate and served herself a small portion before placing it in the stainless steel microwave and nuking it until the cheese bubbled near to bursting.

She reclaimed her meal from the microwave. She knew pasta for breakfast wasn't typical, but nothing about her life was typical at the moment. She stabbed the pasta with her fork before placing it in her mouth.

The tomato sauce and spices hit her first, followed by the texture of the pasta and then the gooiness of the cheese. This was fantastic.

"I see you found the food Bess brought over," Olivia's mother, Kathryn, said as she entered the kitchen.

Bess? As in Olivia's old teacher and her parents' next door neighbor, Bess? Olivia had seen, even through the haze of her own life, something on the news a few weeks back about Bess going through a situation similar to Olivia. Granted, Bess' husband probably hadn't been cheating on her for years. But then again, Olivia's heartbreak had never made it onto the television, so no one was the winner in all of this. How was Bess cooking creations like this so soon after her husband's betrayal? Had she already picked up the pieces of her life?

Olivia had thought about reaching out to Bess when she'd first heard the news because Bess had been so good to her. But then Olivia realized the last thing she wanted was people reaching out to her when Bart told the world about his life back in Seattle, and she decided to leave Bess alone. There were still several texts and voicemails left unread and unheard on her phone. She knew most of them were well-meaning, and a few were likely from people who just wanted to be nosy, but Olivia just couldn't respond to them. They were sure to want to hear that she was okay, and Olivia was anything but okay.

Granted, at the moment, the cheesy pasta was helping a little. And her girls were helping a lot. Enough that she was beginning to think that one day she would maybe be okay. Never healed completely, but maybe okay.

"After you finish that pasta, you should try some of this tiramisu," her mom said as she opened the top of a pan that had been covered with aluminum foil. The sweet smell hit Olivia immediately.

"Um, yeah. That sounds like a great idea," Olivia said as she popped another bite of pasta into her mouth, and her mother beamed.

"Bess is starting a food truck," Kathryn said, and Olivia

nearly dropped her fork. Bess got cheated on and humiliated, and she was going to open a food truck? Whereas Olivia could barely get clothes on each day?

"That's ..." Olivia thought of nearly a dozen words: ambitious, incredible, brave, genius. She landed on, "That's courageous."

"It is," Kathryn said as she sat on the barstool next to Olivia and pulled the cake pan in front of her, going into the entire dessert with a fork. Bart would have been appalled by the lack of manners, so Olivia decided to do the same as her mother. She wished Bart was here to see it.

"You've been courageous as well," Kathryn said after she cleared her mouth of tiramisu.

Olivia wanted to deny what her mother was saying but was too caught up in the taste of the cream and coffee flavors in her mouth. "So good," Olivia said.

Kathryn laughed. "It is. Everything Bess makes is."

Olivia could believe it. But it was time to get back to what her mother had been saying.

"Mom, I ran. How is that courageous?" Olivia asked as she put down her fork. Even Bess' incredible fare wasn't tempting when the ever-present pit in her stomach grew huge.

"Olivia. You picked up your daughters, and you left a situation that has been toxic and abusive for years."

"So why did it take me so long to leave? How did I let my children stay in that? How did I allow myself to become this barely distinguishable copy of the woman I used to be?" Olivia's eyes welled up with tears. She was so sick of crying. How many nights over the last fifteen years had she spent with tears spilling on her pillow?

"Do not go there," Kathryn said, her voice fierce. "You did what you had to."

"Did I, Mom? Because from where I'm standing, I did everything wrong."

Kathryn turned, pulling her daughter into a hug and holding on tight. Olivia's arms fell against her sides; she was unable to wrap them around her mom when she felt so unworthy of the comfort.

"Bart manipulated you and charmed the rest of us. We were all puppets in that devil of a man's show. We should have pulled you out long ago," Kathryn said into Olivia's hair.

Olivia shook her head. "I wouldn't have gone." She pulled back from her mother and looked down at her plate of pasta.

"I know," Kathryn whispered. "But we should have tried."

"I would have pushed you away. And besides, it's so easy to blame yourself in hindsight," Olivia said.

Kathryn nodded. "Wise words from my beautiful, smart, and gracious daughter. Now use some of that mercy you're doling out on us for yourself," Kathryn said as she stood from her stool and walked out of the kitchen.

Was she showing her family mercy? She guessed she was. But who could blame them? These had been her decisions. It wasn't up to them to save her. But then she thought about her own girls and how she would feel if anything horrible happened to either of them. If Rachel or Pearl made a decision that put them right in the same position Olivia was in, would Olivia feel to blame if she couldn't save them? She could see what her mother was saying. And maybe if her mom was right about this, she was right about more. Maybe Olivia could start showing herself a little more mercy.

"MOM, MOM! LOOK AT THIS!" Pearl called out from where

she stood under the monkey bars. As soon as Olivia looked her way, Pearl jumped, catching the closest bar and pulling her way across the set.

"Amazing, Pearl!" Olivia called out from where she sat on a bench under the new spring sun. Late March weather on the island could really be hit or miss. Many days, including that morning, were full of rain. But this afternoon was bursting with brilliant sunshine. And while there was still a definite chill in the air, as long as Olivia stayed out of the shade and in her jacket, it was pretty comfortable to be outside.

"I can do it too," Rachel said as she copied her sister.

Olivia fought the urge to laugh. The girls were always trying to one up the other. Olivia remembered trying to do the same with Dax, but since he was in junior high when she'd barely begun elementary school, there'd been no competition. That never kept Olivia from trying though.

It had been a few weeks since Olivia had begun to start having mercy on herself, and she was finding that mercy gave her new life. Her guilt was still there, but it wasn't a driving force. And she'd begun to realize that her guilt had been crippling her from being what her girls needed, the very thing that had begun the guilt in the first place. If she didn't want to regret today, she needed to put her guilt aside. It was hard, and some days she managed it better than others, but she was trying. And she was a better woman for it.

"Way to go, Rach!" Olivia called out when Rachel punched her arms in the air like an Olympic gymnast after completing the task her sister had.

Both girls then ran for the slide, and Olivia hoped a head-on collision wouldn't occur as they pushed their way to the top.

The barking of a dog caused Olivia to turn away as Rachel slid down the slide with a moping Pearl not even a step behind.

Because of the earlier rain that day and the time of year, the park had been empty when Olivia and the girls had gotten there. She was surprised to hear that others had joined them.

A beautiful brown and white dog was running with its leash trailing behind it, and Olivia giggled as it made its way straight to her. By the goofy grin the dog gave her, Olivia anticipated it was harmless. But she was grateful he'd come to her and not directly to her girls. Both Pearl and Rachel loved any animal, but dogs had a special place in their hearts. They would have tried to cuddle with him, even if he had been about to attack them. Now that Olivia saw that he was harmless, she could smile as she watched her girls jump off the slide and run in her direction. Pearl gave her a triumphant smile when she reached her mother a second before her sister did.

"He's so cute," Rachel said as she rubbed the dog's head, not bothered that she'd lost this time, thanks to the adorable addition to their group.

"He is," Pearl agreed.

Olivia shook her head that the girls could have been at such odds just moments before. Now all was well. Her girls had been going through quite a difficult stage and couldn't seem to find any common ground. It was enough to make Olivia wonder if she should get a dog, but she knew it wouldn't be possible for the time being for the same reason she'd never had one growing up. Her father was horribly allergic to any furry animal.

"Hey there," Olivia said to the dog, noting the unmanned leash. "I'm guessing you must have escaped."

"That he did," a deep voice said from a few feet away.

Olivia and her daughters had been so into the dog that they hadn't noticed another addition to their group.

"Dean?" Olivia was nearly as startled by who the person was as she had been by the sudden voice. She had known the man had been back on the island for the reunion, but she hadn't realized he was back home for another trip so soon. She waited for the soul crushing pain that usually came when Olivia encountered anything or anyone associated with Bart but was filled with relief when it didn't come.

"Hello, Olivia," Dean said as he walked forward and then crouched so that he was level with the girls and the dog before saying, "Good to see you, Rachel, and you too, Pearl."

Without the pain, Olivia was able to genuinely smile. She was surprised that Dean knew the names of her girls. He'd met them just once. Although Dean and Bart had been the best of friends in high school, she knew they hadn't been close for years. So even if Bart had been a bigger part of the girls' lives, she still wouldn't have expected Dean to know their names.

"This is Buster," Dean introduced, and the girls cooed and oohed over their new friend.

"I love him," Pearl declared.

Dean laughed. "I do too."

Olivia realized it had been remiss of her to not introduce Dean to her girls, so she said, "Girls, this is Mr. Haskell. He's a friend of your father."

Dean grimaced for a moment before turning to the girls and giving them each a smile.

"You're friends with our dad?" Rachel asked as she took a step away from Buster.

Olivia was surprised by her daughter's response and realized she needed to fix things.

"I was a long time ago. I'd like to think I was friends with your mom, too. But I left the island right after high school, and we all lost touch," Dean said, giving his full attention to Rachel and seeming to pick up on the subtle hints of animosity she was throwing out.

"Oh," Rachel said, turning to her mom.

"Were you friends with Mr. Haskell too?" she asked.

Olivia didn't hesitate to nod. She'd known Dean practically her whole life, and although they'd never been best friends, she'd always put him in a category of people she could rely on. Before she and Bart had started dating at the beginning of their senior year, she, Bart, and Dean had hung out quite a bit. It was only now that Olivia was realizing that after she'd started dating Bart, those group hangouts had ceased. Either she was with Bart or Dean was with Bart, but never the three of them together.

"So you aren't just dad's friend?" Rachel asked, and Dean nodded.

"Okay," Rachel said before stepping forward to nuzzle Buster once again.

"I hope Buster likes affection," Olivia said as she watched her daughters.

Dean took the seat on the bench next to her. "He loves it," Dean said with a grin as he watched the girls pet and even kiss the dog.

"Oh dear," Olivia said after the kisses. Then she whispered, "They both love dogs so much, but we've never had the chance to get one."

Olivia had hoped that after her children grew out of the needy baby stage that Bart would soften up on his no pet rule, but he'd stood firm. Olivia wasn't sure why he'd cared so much since he was hardly ever at home anyway, but when Bart made a rule, it had to be followed. So her poor girls had begged and put a dog at the top of their Christmas list every year, only to be disappointed every present-opening morning.

"Well, I'm happy to share," Dean whispered back, his grin still lighting up his face.

Olivia realized she knew very little about his life. She knew he'd left the island and had become a successful attorney. But that was all she'd heard. She wondered if there was now a Mrs.

Haskell or a few little Haskells running amok somewhere in Portland. She was pretty sure that was where she'd heard Dean had landed after college.

"As long as you're in town?" Olivia said, remembering that Dean would probably be returning with Buster to Portland sometime soon. The doggy sharing program could only go on for so long.

"I'm actually here now. For good," Dean said as Buster stood, looking like he might take off again. Dean leaned forward to take the handle of the leash back in his hand and turned his attention back to his dog. "Buster is usually pretty obedient. But I think he heard the sound of kids laughing and had to investigate. I must've been slowing him down."

Dean had moved through the former topic of conversation quickly, but his being home for good was big news. Olivia wanted to get back to that but saw Rachel opening her mouth to speak, so she knew she'd have to wait to get more information out of Dean.

"Dogs can run way faster than humans," Rachel said knowingly in response to Dean, eliciting laughter from both of the adults.

Rachel narrowed her eyes at her mother and then Dean, putting an immediate stop to their laughing, when Pearl asked, "Can we play a game with him?"

Rachel seemed to immediately forget about how upset she was and eagerly waited for Dean's reply.

Olivia shared a quick glance with Dean, both of them knowing Pearl had saved them from Rachel's wrath, before Dean grinned at the girls. "If your mom says it's okay."

Olivia nodded, and both girls cheered. Dean took a ball out of his pocket and handed it to Pearl.

"Throw that ball as hard as you can, and Buster will bring it back to you," Dean said as he looked down to unclip the leash from Buster's collar. Pearl threw the ball immediately. Thankfully, Dean was quick, and Buster didn't take the leash with him again as he lunged after the ball.

The girls ran a few feet after him and then stopped, both calling, "Here Buster!"

The sweet dog brought the ball right back to Pearl who threw it again.

"Hey!" Rachel said, and Olivia knew the argument before she heard it.

"Pearl, next time it's Rachel's turn, and keep taking turns or I'm giving that ball back to Mr. Haskell," Olivia said, and both girls nodded.

Buster ran the ball back to Pearl, but she handed it to her sister, causing Rachel to smile before she threw the ball. Man, she wished she could bottle up this magical getting along and bring it home.

"So you're home for good?" Olivia asked as she leaned back in her seat, ready to get back to the conversation point that Dean had moved past so quickly. She was surprised and also a little curious to hear the news, considering Dean had always been the type to want to conquer the world.

Dean nodded. "I guess I'm an island guy at heart," he said, and Olivia smiled, thinking the same thing about herself. She enjoyed a weekend or even a longer vacation away, but this was home.

"Are you still a big, bad attorney?" Olivia teased.

Dean laughed. "I don't know about the big and bad part, but yes. I started my own firm in Portland a few years ago and built up a pretty decent client list. It's relatively easy to work remotely since I do estate planning. I'll fly back for court about once a month, but other than that, nothing was really holding me there," Dean said as he watched the girls. This time Pearl's ball hadn't gone very far, and she was demanding a rethrow. Surprisingly, Rachel gave it to her.

From the way Dean wouldn't look at Olivia to his tone, she was pretty sure there was more behind what he was saying. But Olivia had plenty of her own stuff she'd prefer not to share, so a light conversation between old friends to catch up on the simple surface events in life was just what she needed.

"How old are the girls now?" Dean asked another safe question, and Olivia wanted to hug him, she was so grateful.

By this point in a conversation, even the most well-meaning of people would have started to pry into her living situation or Bart's. However, Dean seemed content to just sit beside her and talk about her favorite subject of conversation: her adorable daughters. Maybe it was because he'd already gotten Bart's side of the story, but Olivia doubted it. Dean and Bart hadn't been close in so long. Olivia knew the men in town who Bart had confided in. They were obviously not Team Olivia and even went out of their way to avoid her. Dean's relaxed manner beside her told her he hadn't chosen a side, and for that, Olivia couldn't be more grateful.

"Rachel is nine and Pearl is seven," Olivia said proudly. She honestly didn't know how she would have survived these past couple of months without her girls. Heck, how she would have survived the past nine years.

"They're beautiful," Dean said, and something about the way he said it made Olivia feel sad for her friend.

"Thank you," Olivia said with what she hoped was a gracious smile.

Then Dean added, "Rachel is your spitting image, but the way Pearl is determined to get the ball out of those bushes reminds me of a little girl I knew once upon a time."

Olivia laughed because she'd thought the same thing many a time. Olivia had had a stubborn streak a mile wide as a child and even a teen. She'd become more subdued over the years, but there'd been a time when she would have been in the bushes right beside her daughter if the ball had been her goal. What were Olivia's goals now? Where had that determination gone?

Olivia's smile fell, and Dean glanced her way, sensing she'd gone somewhere other than where their conversation had taken them. As they sat in silence, he seemed content to let her work it out.

"So where are you setting up house?" Olivia finally asked when some of her disappointment in herself subsided. She was supposed to be showing herself mercy, but it was an everyday struggle.

"I bought a place on Letman's Cove." Dean named the same cove where she was now living in her parents' home.

"Really?" Olivia asked, assuming he knew she was back home after separating from Bart. Since it was the same home she'd lived in when they'd been friends years ago, he had to know they were now fellow Letman Cove residents. "I haven't seen you around, neighbor," she said as she nudged his shoulder.

"The sale went through about a month back, but I've been tying up loose ends in Portland. This is my first week back home fulltime," Dean said.

Olivia got loose ends. She felt like she was going to be tying them up from her marriage for the rest of her life. She had finally opened up her own bank account the week before. Not that she had much to put in the account. But it was there, with just Olivia Penn as an account owner. She'd thought about keeping her married name to have it stay the same as her daughters. But she realized it was more important for her to sever the connection with Bart than to keep the same name as her daughters. They would hopefully understand her decision someday.

"Which home?" Olivia asked. There were only eight homes on the small cove. As she asked the question, Olivia, even through her grief-induced haze, suddenly recalled a For Sale sign in front of one of them a few weeks back. The cute green and white beach house must have been the home Dean had bought.

"The Arnold's place, two doors down from Bess, right?" Olivia answered since she'd suddenly remembered.

Dean smiled. "Exactly. I've loved the houses on the cove since high school," he said.

"Are you trying to say you were jealous of me back then?" Olivia teased.

Dean laughed. "Something like that. My mom told me about the Arnolds selling, and I had to try for it. I wasn't planning on moving back so soon. But sometimes things just work out the way they're supposed to," Dean said with a shrug.

Olivia wasn't sure she believed that. Nothing in her life had worked out the way it was supposed to. She had never thought she'd be a single mom back in her childhood bedroom. But she was glad things were working out for one of them.

"It's adorable," Olivia said about the home.

Dean nodded. "But it needs a whole lot of work."

Olivia could imagine. The Arnolds had been the "older couple" on her street, even back when she was in high school. She knew they had moved from their home to a senior center. Because of their age, she imagined it was hard for them to keep up on the work a beach home needed. The constant salty air and flipping sand could be rough on a house. Her parents hated that part of owning a cove home, but the view more than made up for it.

"Mom! I'm hungry!" Rachel whined as she ran toward where Olivia sat on the bench beside Dean. It would never cease to amaze her that her children could go from having a good time to being about to keel over from lack of food within seconds. But she knew better than to make them wait when they got to this point. "Hanger" was a real monster.

"Rachel, what did I say about whining?" Olivia asked. Even if her daughter was on the verge of hanger, she needed to mind her manners.

"Mom, can we please go?" Rachel changed her tone, and Olivia smiled proudly at her daughter.

"Of course. Let's gather up Pearly girl and we can walk home," Olivia said.

Rachel ran off to tell her sister that mom said they had to leave.

"It was good to see you again, Dean," Olivia said honestly. She wouldn't have thought seeing a man who had been such good friends with Bart would have been nice, but it was. He'd been the perfect conversation companion that day.

"It's good to see you too, Liv." Dean used the nickname he'd had for her back in high school, and she realized no one had called her Liv in years. She missed it.

"I guess we'll keep seeing one another around. Let me know if you need anything," Olivia said.

Dean nodded. "Thanks. Same to you. It's been a really good time to move into the neighborhood now that Mrs. Wilder is opening her food truck. I haven't eaten so well in years," Dean said as he patted his flat stomach.

Olivia laughed. The entire neighborhood was enjoying the fruits of Bess' labor.

"I guess I need to call her Bess now that we're all adults, but isn't it weird? I still imagine her as our senior English teacher," Dean said.

Olivia nodded. "It took me a few years as well, but Gen and I becoming better friends made it easier," Olivia said.

"Oh right. I almost forgot Gen and Mrs.—I mean, Bess are sisters," Dean said.

"Mo-om!" Rachel called out.

"I really better go, but see ya around, Dean," Olivia said, and she couldn't help her giant grin as she walked away from the park bench. She was beginning to feel a little bit more alive every day and could finally imagine a day when the hurt in her heart for what she had lost would be replaced with the hope of something better.

EIGHT

DEB SAT BACK in her chair as she surveyed the landscape painting she'd been working on for the past few weeks. She was close to done, but there was something that just wasn't right. She hated it when things went wrong so late in her work. This was the point when everything should be coming together. It was almost too late to change anything, but she had to try. Maybe it was the amount of pink in the sky of the sunset? Should there be more purple?

Cracking her neck, Deb stood and walked toward her studio windows that let in so much light. Now that the days were getting longer, Deb had much more time every day to paint. In the winter, she often only had a few hours a day between sunrise and sunset where the light was just right for her painting. But now that it was officially spring, sunshine was prevalent for quite a few more hours, and Deb was able to be more productive in her work.

Deb watched as a man walked a dog along the beach that bordered her backyard. The rocky beach was quite a bit more used and less secluded than the cove that Bess' home backed onto, but Deb would take her beautiful beach, even if it meant dealing with rock hunting tourists and many, many more neighbors.

Watching the man walk, Deb stretched and wondered if she ought to go out for her daily run. But she decided to wait until twilight and make use of the light while she had it.

She turned and walked back to her chair, sitting down and staring at her painting. She focused on the purple on her palette and dipped a brush into it before looking over her work one more time. She had to be sure about the purple because once it was on the canvas, there was no turning back.

As she gazed at the painting of the sunset on the beautiful sandy beach that looked so much like Bess' cove—when she'd first started the work, she'd arranged a set of white chairs on Bess' back porch and had used that view as her inspiration for her newest work—she wondered if maybe the painting was just right. Maybe she was the one who had the issues. In her years as an artist, one thing Deb had learned was sometimes everything about the art could be right, but if something was wrong with her, it could mess with the way she saw her art.

She bit her nail as she thought about Bess. Was that what she was worried about? But Bess was doing so much better. Better than she should've been. Deb still wasn't sure why she hadn't started with divorce proceedings and kicked Jon permanently to the curb, but the rest of Bess' life was thriving. The news and its surrounding gossip had blown over quickly—Bess' non-reaction to the whole thing had worked wonders—and she was well on her way to owning her own business. Deb knew Bess was scared to death, but she was also alive in a way Deb had never seen. Bess lit up with talk of the food truck and now knew things like how to get a business license. She'd bought a used, well-cared-for truck a few weeks ago and was working hard on remodeling it with help from her oldest son, Stephen. He'd taken a vacation to help his mom for the past few weeks, and for that, she knew Bess was immensely grateful. In fact, Deb wanted to go up to Bess' tonight since Stephen would be on his way back to Seattle early the next morning.

Without any more thought about her painting, Deb put her brush up and suddenly added purple to the sunset. She began to blend the color in with the pinks and oranges from her palette as her thoughts once again strayed.

Bess wasn't the issue in Deb's life. Although she was still worried for her friend, she knew Bess would come out of this stronger than she'd ever been. So what was nagging at her?

Wes had called her the day before and, although he was feeling slightly bogged down by a project for his history class, his life was going swimmingly. Bailee was excelling in school and had recently been offered admission into three of her top picks for college. Deb hoped she would choose something close to home, University of Washington had always been Bailee's number one choice, but who knew with that girl? She was a bit fickle when it came to decision making. And once Bailee was gone ...

Deb pinpointed her reason for unrest. What was she going to do next year?

Rich hadn't been home since that week-long trip a couple of months back, and Deb knew it was because he was busy with flights. She had a tracker on her phone that told her where he was at every moment of every day, and Rich had flown between London and New York over a dozen times, along with numerous shorter US and European trips.

Although he *had* had a few days at a time in London between those trips. Deb had been waiting for Rich to tell her he was going to take one of those breaks on Whisling, but he hadn't.

Part of her knew she should just ask her husband to come home, tell him she missed him, but part of her didn't think she should have to. Why didn't he want to be here as much as she wanted him to?

Had the distance been a mistake? Things had been different between the two of them on Rich's most recent trip home. It was almost as if a barrier had been built up between Deb and Rich, and Deb couldn't help but think it had to be this distance.

Should she have uprooted her life and her daughter? Well, it was too late to dwell on that now, but where should she go from here?

Deb looked at her app and found that Rich was at home. She should call him, put these feelings of unease at rest. She looked at her clock. Because it was early afternoon in Washington, it would be pretty close to bedtime in London. That should work.

Deb dialed her husband and waited for the phone to begin ringing. It rang twice before she heard the sound of Rich picking up.

"Hello?" a female voice said, and Deb pulled her phone away from her ear to make sure she had indeed dialed Rich's number. She had.

Her heart dropped to her stomach. What was a woman doing answering Rich's phone? At almost ten pm, no less? She knew he wasn't at work, so what was going on?

Deb took a deep breath, relaxing herself. There could be any number of explanations for this. Although Deb couldn't think of a single one.

She needed to speak.

"Hi. I'm calling for Rich," Deb said, somehow not allowing the fear and aggravation she felt to enter her voice.

"Right. Just a moment," the woman said, and Deb listened carefully as the woman left the phone. What background noises did she hear? Maybe the woman was a colleague and the two of them were out to a late dinner right near Rich's home? But Deb had been sure the dot that was Rich on her app was *at* his home, not near it.

It took over a minute for the woman to get Rich, and Deb had too much time to think. What excuse did Rich have for a woman at his home so late in the evening? And why was he so far away from his phone? What was taking him so long to answer?

"Deb," Rich said, sounding a little out of breath. What was going on? Where had Rich been?

"It's good to hear from you," Rich added.

"Is it?" Deb couldn't help the snide remark. But how would Rich feel if Deb had a man over at ten at night.

"Deb." Rich's tone held warning, but Deb didn't care. It was her turn to be warning him.

"Don't *Deb* me. What the hell is going on, Rich? Why is a woman answering your phone in your house at ten o'clock at night?" Deb felt her tone of voice rising, but she didn't care. Rich deserved her wrath, didn't he?

"Deb, calm down," Rich said. Then off the phone he said, "Halley, would you give me a minute?"

Deb hated that he'd taken time to speak to Halley or seemed to care about Halley's circumstances at all when his first and foremost concern should be Deb. So what if Halley could hear Deb lose it? Shouldn't Rich be focused on his wife?

"Halley is my nutritionist," Rich said back into the phone, and Deb could tell by his voice that he was walking. "My work schedule has been crazy this week, and I had to ask her to come over later than normal for our weekly session."

"Nutritionists don't do home sessions," Deb said. This was an excuse that reeked of something fishy.

"Halley does," Rich responded.

Deb could just imagine him holding the bridge of his nose in frustration. Well good, because Deb was frustrated as well. "Why doesn't she sound like a Brit?" Deb asked.

"What?"

"If she lives in London, shouldn't she have an accent?"

"She's an American living in London. Like me," Rich said.

Deb guessed that made sense. But ten pm?

"Deb, things have been crazy. I took over trips for two of my coworkers, and I'm just on the verge of having too many hours. You know how exhausted that makes me," Rich said, sounding like he was trying to get off the phone. Oh no he didn't.

"But not too exhausted to have your nutritionist come over," Deb said.

"This is important," Rich said.

And a call with his wife wasn't?!

"Why did she answer your phone?" Deb asked, feeling like she was losing her mind. Something wasn't right about this, yet Rich had an answer for every one of her questions. Weird answers, but answers, nonetheless.

"I was climbing up to a top cabinet to see if I had any of the almond flour she was suggesting for my diet this week. I heard my phone ring, thought it could be work and urgent, and asked her to grab it," Rich said.

"Then why did it take you so long to get to the phone?" Deb asked.

"Because I had to climb down, Deb. Are we almost through with the third degree?" Rich asked.

Deb wasn't sure. "How would you feel if I had a man over at ten pm answering my phone?" she asked.

"Is he your nutritionist?" Rich asked.

The sarcasm in his voice was hard to miss.

"I really should go, Deb. Halley is doing me a huge favor by coming over after hours," Rich said.

Deb shook her head, knowing something was wrong. Why

didn't Rich just kick his nutritionist out and try to make things right with his wife living an ocean and a continent away? Why did he care so much about his nutritionist's feelings? Granted, if she was doing him a favor, Rich was the type to feel indebted. But ... Deb wasn't sure what her but was, but she had one.

"Rich," Deb began.

"I'll call you later," Rich said and then hung up.

Deb pulled the phone away from her ear, staring at the black screen. Rich had just hung up on her.

DEB SAT in front of her computer, her painting all but forgotten. Her daughter had come home from school and then gone back out to spend the night at her best friend's home.

Deb was all alone in her house as she looked at the clock that read ten pm. Yes, it wouldn't be normal to have a man over at this time. Even if he was her nutritionist.

She'd spent the hours since her call with Rich snooping. She knew it wasn't what healthy relationships were built on, but Deb was feeling less and less trust in her husband.

When he'd come home with his clothes folded in his suitcase, Deb had ignored the red flag. When he hadn't kissed her for too long, again she'd excused his behavior away. And then there was the fact that he hadn't even tried to come home again since that trip, a big problem in and of itself. But now with Halley in his house at ten at night, Deb would be an idiot not to try to connect the dots, right? Was she going nuts? Was her worry that her marriage would end like Bess' driving her to find skeletons where there weren't any? Or was her gut right on point?

That last thought had driven her to her husband's bank account. She figured she might find something through his activity on there. And she'd found something all right. Rich had changed his bank login information, so Deb was locked out.

Deb and Rich had kept separate personal bank accounts for their entire marriage. Some found it odd, but Deb hadn't cared. It worked for them. There were a few years when Deb hadn't worked while they were in the middle of having young children, so Rich had covered their costs of living. But other than that short time, Deb had always worked. So whatever each of them made was theirs. They had a few joint accounts where they would keep their money for family costs, but then whatever was left over was fair game. It had kept them from arguing over the small things like Rich wanting a TV for the den that Deb didn't think was necessary. When he had bought it with his money, Deb had been fine with it. Besides making their marriage far less tense, it made taxes easier for them as well.

But now Deb had to wonder, was this just another piece of the distance between them? And why was Rich changing his login information? They'd never locked one another out of their financial situations.

In a panic, Deb went to her account to make sure everything was still there. She wasn't sure when or how she'd come to accept the fact that her husband might try to steal her money. But Rich was keeping secrets, his bank account login was proof of that, and Deb was beginning to wonder if he was still the same man she'd loved for over twenty years.

Her money was still just where it should be, but Deb decided to change her login info as well. Better safe than sorry. If all of her suspicions were wrong, man she hoped she was just being crazy, she was sure she and Rich would have a laugh about it someday. But today it all felt very real, and Deb needed to stop ignoring her gut.

She next went to his social media accounts, sure she'd be

locked out again. But she easily entered his username and pass-word, getting in.

Okay. Not what she was expecting.

Nothing seemed amiss in his social media accounts, and Deb began to wonder if she was overreacting? She honestly felt like she was losing her mind. One minute she was sure she shouldn't and couldn't trust Rich, but the next ...

She reviewed all of the red flags and told herself she wasn't being paranoid. This was strange. She wanted to call Bess to go over things with her, but even though her best friend was doing so much better, she didn't need a paranoid friend to add to her already full plate. Besides, this was her last night with Stephen. Something Deb was missing. But she was sure Bess would understand.

Deb rubbed a hand over her makeupless face, unsure of where to go from here. Maybe onto dating websites to try to find if Rich was ... what? Trying to get a date? That seemed absurd. But Deb had read enough books and watched enough true crime to know that kind of stuff happened.

If he wasn't on those sites, would it prove anything? But if he was, it would prove ... Deb felt sick to her stomach. Could she do this? And yet she couldn't not do this.

The name of a woman Deb knew as a flight attendant suddenly sprang to her mind. Carla Derringer. She knew from conversations with Rich that Carla still worked for their airline and was often on the same flights as Rich. She and Deb had reconnected a couple of years before because Carla had wanted to throw a surprise party for her husband, and she and Rich had been involved. Carla was a flight attendant based in New York, not London, but maybe she would know something? Or, even though they hadn't been close in years, she could be a friend and ease Deb's worries?

But would the call get back to Rich? She knew if it did, Rich would be livid. Deb wasn't the kind of woman who checked up on her husband, and Rich would hate that she'd come to this. But she had to know. She'd deal with Rich's wrath if she had to, but she couldn't live with the questions that kept swirling. She needed some answers.

Deb looked at the clock, knowing it would be after one am in New York. But if Carla was still a flight attendant, who knew where she was and what time zone she was in. Deb figured she could text.

Deb's phone rang almost immediately after texting Carla to see if she was up, and Deb drew in a deep breath before answering. Deb wasn't sure what she was going to say but hoped she'd feel guided when the time came.

"Deb," Carla said as soon as Deb answered.

"Hi, Carla. Sorry to call out of the blue like this," Deb said.

"Oh no. I'm so glad you did. It's been too long," Carla said, and Deb had to agree. She already felt calmer than she had before the call.

"It's like one am in New York, isn't it?" Deb asked as she sat up on her couch. The nervousness of what she was about to ask hit her hard, and the anxiety that accompanied it wouldn't let Deb relax.

"I'm on a layover in Dubai and just got up from a nap, so it's perfect timing," Carla said.

Deb remembered those days. She didn't miss getting too much of her sleep in random snatches of time.

"Are you still based in New York?" Deb asked, thinking small talk was the way to go until she got her nerve up to ask Carla ... what would she ask? Deb tried to focus on Carla's response instead of how Deb would derail the conversation in just a few minutes.

"I am. But my husband is thinking about early retirement and wants me to think about it too. Our kids have all moved back down to Earl's hometown in Georgia, and Earl wants to be near them," Carla explained.

Deb couldn't blame Earl. "Will you miss the flying?" she asked, feeling that was the polite thing to do.

"I will. It's been a pretty awesome career to be able to travel the world like this. But I will enjoy getting a full night's sleep every night, and I won't miss the drama," Carla said.

Something about the way she said drama made Deb's heart drop.

"Deb," Carla said slowly, and Deb knew in her gut what was coming. She and Carla may not have been close for a long time, but there were some things about your friends you didn't forget. Like the way they delivered bad news.

"I'm calling about Rich," Deb said as she felt tears filling her eyes.

"I know," Carla said, her voice breaking. "I wasn't sure what to do when I heard."

"So it's true?" Deb asked.

Carla cleared her throat. "Rich is having an affair, Deb," Carla said and then let out a sob.

Deb felt her body go weak. She had to lie down. She shifted on the couch so that she could lie down, but she had to hear more.

"You know more, don't you," Deb said.

"Deb, are you sure you want to hear this?" Carla said as she sniffled.

Deb felt herself nod. "I need to know everything, and Rich is telling me nothing."

"I found out about a month ago. She's one of us," Carla said, the disgust in her voice easy to hear. "She's younger than we are and was bragging to her friends in the crew room about her new pilot boyfriend. I've worked a few flights with her before and she's ... well not very easy to work with."

Carla was one of the nicest people Deb knew, so this was about as cruel of an insult as Carla would say.

"What's her name?" Deb asked.

"Halley," Carla said, and Deb just shook her head. She knew it. And Rich had acted as if Deb was crazy instead of telling her the truth. The hurt began to give way to a terrible wave of anger that took over Deb's body.

She sat up again.

"What else, Carla?" Deb commanded. She wanted every tiny detail. She wanted to throw each fact in Rich's face so he knew exactly why she would be leaving him forever. "Is she the reason for his transfer to London?"

Had it been going on that long? Hurt threatened to return, but Deb unleashed her anger on it.

"I did some digging around after I overheard what Halley had said. I wasn't just going to take some girl's word that a man I've known for twenty years isn't anything like the person I thought he was. You know Rich and Earl have stayed friends over the years," Carla said, and Deb nodded. It was Carla and Deb who'd introduced the men. But when Deb had stopped flying, it'd become hard to keep the friendship going since, about that same time, Carla's trips stopped taking her cross country to Washington. She now almost always just traveled east of New York. But since Rich had still been doing many flights between the west and east coasts, he'd often see Earl on his New York layovers.

"So I asked Earl what he knew. He told me he suspected as much, but when he tried to talk to Rich, Rich exploded and told Earl if he could suspect this of Rich, they were no longer friends," Carla said.

Deb could completely imagine that conversation since Rich had given her the same stiff arm.

"When was this?" Deb asked. Answers. She needed more answers.

"In early January," Carla said.

That fit Deb's timeline. Things had been going well with Rich, even with the distance, until about the holidays. She and Earl must have noticed the changes in Rich about the same time.

"After talking to Earl, I couldn't let it go. I talked to a few of my friends who worked with Halley often, and they confirmed that the flights they'd worked with Halley and Rich were ..."

"Just tell me Carla."

"It began with just flirting, but you know Rich. He's charming. My friends thought nothing of it. Then Rich and Halley began leaving flights together. According to my friends, they didn't try too hard to hide things," Carla said softly.

Deb felt her throat clogging with emotion, but now wasn't the time. She had a chance to get more answers, and she had to have them.

"They're living together," Carla said, and Deb felt her body go so weak she was worried she'd drop the phone.

Living together?

"I'm so sorry, Deb," Carla said, and Deb knew her friend really was. "I wasn't sure of things until earlier this week. I wanted to call, but I just didn't know ... as soon as I saw your text...."

"I know your place isn't a fun one either, Carla. Thank you for your honesty," Deb said, but that was all she could do. She was well and truly drained. "Bye, Carla."

Deb hung up, unable to feel anything other than the wave after wave of anger that was hitting her. How could Rich do this to her? And then act as if this was all in her mind? His nutritionist?

Several names she would be happy to call Rich flitted through her mind, but Deb knew calling him now and reaming him out would only feel good for that moment. He'd been living a lie for months and hadn't had the decency to tell her the truth, even after she'd caught him red-handed. Revenge would be a lot more than just an upset phone call. Because now, Rich would pay.

NINE

"I DON'T WANT him to come over," Stephen said as he sat on the couch with Bess. He sounded as petulant as he had as a child, and Bess would've smiled at the memories if the *him* Stephen didn't want to see wasn't his father.

Stephen had been visiting Bess for the last two weeks, a Godsend for her soul and her "new" food truck. Stephen had always been a whiz when it came to anything handy, and so now her truck was outfitted with brand new appliances on the inside and boasted a fresh coat of vibrant red paint and the name of her new business, Scratch Made by Bess, on the outside. Seeing her name on the truck had finally helped to make the whole experience feel real. Bess was doing this, and she was unbelievably excited.

"He hasn't seen you in months," Bess said as she moved over to pat her son on the knee. Stephen had always been the most stubborn of her children. It meant when he became determined, things got done. But on the flip side, when he became determined, things didn't get done. It all just depended on Stephen's mindset.

Stephen had always been a daddy's boy. Bess liked to joke

that as soon as the umbilical cord was cut, Stephen jumped into his dad's arms and never left them again. Stephen took the news that his hero wasn't as infallible as he'd thought the hardest of their children. She knew James and Lindsey often had lunch with their father since they were all in the city, but Stephen hadn't been answering Jon's calls, and Jon was worried about their oldest son. Jon and Bess might not see eye to eye on their marriage—Bess still wasn't sure what she wanted as far as a future with Jon—but they would continue to put their children above their own issues. And Bess knew Stephen needed his dad.

"It's been that way for a reason. I don't want to see him," Stephen said as he crossed his arms across his broad chest and shook his head.

"Stephen, he's your father," Bess said softly. "That is never going to change."

"I get that, Mom. I really do. I know you think this is another 'Stephen acting like a stubborn and willful child' moment, but it's not. Jon Wilder is my father. He raised me and all of that, but the man I knew isn't there anymore. I have to come to terms with that before I can see him." Stephen was stoic as he spoke, but Bess could see that his heart had been broken, and she hated Jon for that.

"I broke off my engagement with Jana," Stephen said, and Bess' eyes went wide.

Bess had no idea. She knew Stephen had been evasive when she'd asked about the woman he'd dated for five years and had been engaged to for the last six months. When Bess had asked if Jana would be okay with Stephen being gone for two weeks, he'd just laughed and said it was fine. She had no idea that that laughter had been hiding something so distressing. Why hadn't he said anything?

"When?" Bess asked, trying to keep her thoughts from

running wild when what she needed to do was focus on Stephen.

"About a month ago. So when you asked me to come and help you, it was exactly what I needed," Stephen said lightly. But his tone didn't fool his mother. Bess just gripped her son's knee tighter. How he must be hurting.

"Why, Stephen?"

"Dad," Stephen whispered. He sat up straight to add, "You've heard the countless times people have said I'm exactly like him."

Bess nodded. Her son and husband both loved all sports with baseball being their favorite. The two were also literature fanatics. Stephen was actually in the middle of writing his dissertation for his PhD in British Literature so that he could teach British literature like his dad was doing. Bess should have seen this and known this would be yet another reason why Stephen would take the news harder than her other children. Resilience had never been Stephen's strong suit, and with all of this, he had lost so much.

"So what if I *am* exactly like him? I can't do what he did to you to Jana. It would kill me to hurt her like that. It kills me that he hurt you like that." Tears welled up in Stephen's eyes that he quickly swiped away, but it was too late. The tears were coursing down Bess' face, and there was no stopping her and her son from having the talk they needed.

"You *are* a lot like your father. You are both determined to do good in the world, and you are both smart. So smart. You both make me laugh, and you both like to wear chinos," Bess said, making her son chuckle, the exact reason for her last remark.

"But Stephen. Can you imagine your father doing what you did these past couple of weeks? He hates anything to do with remodeling, although he did plenty of it while we were married, for my sake. When the going got tough, he would have begged me to hire out the work instead of the two of us taking it on. But you and I took it on. And smashed it, if I do say so myself."

Stephen had stopped laughing but was still smiling.

"I see what you're saying, Mom. But our core values are so similar. What if deep down I'm a cheater too?" Stephen asked, his smile dropping from his face.

"Nothing in your father's core values condones what he did. He went against everything that he knew and admired when he made that terrible mistake. It was why it was so surprising and hit us so hard. This isn't like your dad. And even though I am still so angry and hurt by what he did, I won't allow this one action to define him. He was so much more than that, and he still can be. I know he's working hard on forgiving himself," Bess said.

Stephen nodded before asking, "Has he apologized to you?"

Bess let out a laugh that kind of sounded like a snort. "Yes. Many, many times."

"So he's sorry?" Stephen asked.

"So very sorry. I think. It's hard to trust him now, but that's my issue to deal with," Bess said.

"Except it's not, Mom. I get that you're trying to protect us, but I'm an adult. We all are. I'm glad to know that Dad apologized, and I'm even more glad to know that you're making him work to gain your trust back. You've always been too good to us. I'm happy that you're looking out for you in this situation."

Was that what Bess was doing? She guessed she was, and she was grateful that her son could see that it was a good thing for her.

"I know that you're an adult, and I'm grateful that we are having this conversation. There were things I needed to hear, and I now know there were things you needed to know. But that doesn't change that no matter what I decide, Jon Wilder is your father. He will always be your father. I won't push you, but if you need help working through this situation, I'm here," Bess said, keeping eye contact with her son as she said every word.

Stephen nodded. "And know that I'm here too, Mom. The door opens both ways."

Bess gave her son a small smile. Most days she was fully aware that her little boy was now a man, embarking on a career and making huge life decisions. But some days, like in that moment, it was hard for her to believe that Stephen was so grown up that he was now wanting to take care of her. He had always had the biggest heart.

"I'll keep that in mind, Son. Thank you. Now back to you, Stephen. I get that you're trying to work out your feelings for your dad, and I respect that. But Jana? We need to talk about her. You might be an adult now, but I get to meddle in your life forever." Bess said the last sentence with a grin, hoping it would get her son to open up.

"Is that what they teach you in Mom 101?" Stephen asked.

Bess laughed. "201. The basic course couldn't handle that kind of commitment."

This time Stephen laughed at his mom, and Bess waited for him to finish and finally really talk to her. She couldn't believe they'd worked side by side for two weeks and he'd said nothing about Jana. Now that he'd told her the truth, Bess realized that she had noticed that every time she'd brought Jana up, his answers had been to the point and he'd move on to another subject. But he hadn't said or done anything to make Bess think they were over. She had merely assumed he must be missing her and didn't want to dwell on that.

"Jana and I had already been going through some rough patches, so I can't blame everything on Dad. It wasn't like we came to dinner that night, and after you told us about Dad, I went home and broke up with her."

"I was guessing it's a little more complex than that," Bess said softly, prompting her son to tell her more.

"She's a really good person," Stephen said as he leaned back onto the couch and scrubbed his hands over his face.

Bess nodded. She knew that. She'd come to love Jana like one of her own.

"But I was spending so much time researching and writing for my dissertation. And I think she was starting to feel neglected. I would continue to promise date nights or that I'd finally take time off, but the dissertation seemed so pressing, it consumed my world. She was understanding for the first few months, but after the whole thing with Dad, escaping to my dissertation was all I ever did anymore. I knew it. Jana knew it. When it had just been about the pressure of the paper, she was able to live with me blowing her off. But I stopped talking to her about everything, especially you and Dad. She pulled me out of the library one night. It was late. I hadn't called her or returned her texts all day, and she said she was worried about me. She wanted to talk about Dad. The pressure had been building for so long, and I finally exploded. I told her we were done." Stephen paused. "You should have seen her face, Mom. She stepped back from me as if I'd hit her or something. It was literally the most terrible feeling in the world."

By this time, tears were falling from Stephen's eyes, and Bess couldn't help but cry tears with him. Her poor boy. And poor Jana.

"But I couldn't take it back. I knew it was the right thing. I'm a mess. I don't even have it in me to love myself anymore. I can't love someone else. So I let her walk away."

Bess pulled her son into a hug she was sure he thought he was too old for, but he was still her first baby. She let Stephen cry in her arms, and she didn't say a word.

When Stephen pulled away a few minutes later, his tears

were dry and he looked resolved to take on the world once again.

"I'm sorry," Bess said.

Stephen shook his head. "This is all on Dad. You have nothing to be sorry for," he said.

"Oh, I do. I'm sorry that I didn't see this sooner. I'm sorry that you felt the need to be strong and keep this from me. But most of all, I'm so sorry that you are hurting. I hate that you're hurting." Bess kept the tears at bay only because she knew Stephen would hate them.

"I know, Mom. That's why I couldn't tell you. I couldn't add anything else to this terrible situation. This is my stuff. I'll get over it."

Or he wouldn't. Bess was worried about her oldest son. And if he stopped talking to her now, she was worried he'd clam up for good again.

"We don't have our own stuff, Stephen. We're family," Bess said, and Stephen nodded before giving her a half smile that told her he would be okay. Something she'd learned the hard way over the past few months was that hurting now didn't mean he'd always hurt. And things like this wouldn't and couldn't be fixed in a night. But she had an idea as to how Stephen could get some of the help he needed.

"Maybe you should talk to a professional? Especially if you don't feel up to talking to me," Bess said. She didn't add her other thought that he would especially need someone now since Jana wasn't around for him to talk to. Stephen had a decent support network in the city, but she doubted any of his friends were up to the task of helping him sort out his life and feelings.

"Like a shrink?" Stephen asked.

Bess nodded. "Why not? I've started seeing one here, and she's really helped me to sort things out. She's helped me to see that even though my life has fallen to pieces that might be too broken to put back together, I can create new ones when I'm ready. Like this food truck."

Stephen smiled, and Bess knew how proud he was of her. He hadn't stopped telling her for the past two weeks.

"Okay," Stephen said, and Bess knew that was as good of a commitment as she'd get.

"Okay," Bess said and smiled.

The doorbell rang, and Stephen looked at her in a panic.

"You won't have to see him. I'll send him away," Bess said since they both knew the person at the door was Jon. Both Gen and Deb, Bess' two frequent visitors, would have simply walked in the house. Jon knew not to breach Bess' territory anymore. Which was weird in and of itself, considering this had been his home for years. But things were different now.

"I think I'm going to head to bed. I'm leaving on the first ferry tomorrow," Stephen said.

Bess nodded. "I love you, Stephen," she said as she stood with him and pulled him into one last hug.

"I love you, Mom."

Stephen pulled away and walked down the hall toward his bedroom that Bess couldn't bear to change. She wanted her children to always feel they had a home in her home. She'd been hoping to open it to her grandchildren someday soon, but with Stephen breaking off his engagement, that day seemed like it would now be later rather than sooner.

She really hoped he'd be okay. Anger at the situation and at the man on the other side of the door welled up in her as the doorbell rang once again, causing Bess to move to the front door. She took her jacket from the front closet before opening the door and then closing it right behind her.

"Bess," Jon said wistfully as she stood in front of the door and slipped her arms into her jacket. Thanks to the unfolding of spring, the days were getting warmer. But even the warmest of days gave way to chillier nights when one lived so close to the ocean.

"Jon," Bess said, trying to keep her voice steady. She'd seen her husband a handful of times in the past three months, but each time was still so hard. This was the man she'd woken up to for the last thirty years, and now she saw him approximately once a month. It was a future she hadn't expected, and she was still reeling from having to live it.

Jon looked at the door behind Bess and her jacket.

"He won't see me," Jon said, his eyes falling to the ground. And as much as Bess wanted to jump on his sorrow and add to it because she was just that angry, she couldn't. Maybe Jon deserved to lose everything because of what he'd done, but Bess wouldn't revel in his consequences. It wasn't in her nature.

"He's working stuff out, Jon."

Jon nodded. "I know. I got a visit from a very angry Jana. She blames me for everything."

"She has every right to," Bess said.

"She does," Jon answered immediately.

"So you kept your job?" Bess asked, and Jon nodded again.

"The media tried to portray the situation differently, but she was my aide, not my student. An employee of the University, the same as me. Thankfully, only local news picked up the story, and it didn't stay in the limelight for very long. The repercussions for the school and, therefore, me weren't bad. So although I was reamed out by the dean and the administration, they couldn't fire me. Yet. But they aren't happy."

Hearing Jon talk about the other woman even in this context shredded Bess' stomach, and she wanted to cover her ears. But she fought the urge and said what she knew she had to.

"I'm pretty sure no one has come out of this situation happy," Bess said as she thought about her son who was probably struggling to sleep just a few feet away. Granted, Stephen had made his own decisions as well. But Bess couldn't help but think everything had only blown up in their son's face because of Jon.

"I know I'm not," Jon said as he sat on the swing that had graced their front porch since they'd moved in. Bess walked to the white wooden railing of their front porch so that she could lean her back against it as she faced Jon.

"Are you?" Jon asked Bess.

Bess felt startled by the question she had failed to ask herself. Was she? A month ago she would have answered that question with a resounding no. And tonight after her talk with Stephen, it was again a no. But yesterday when she'd been out in the truck with Stephen, gazing over all they'd accomplished, she had been happy. Really happy.

"It depends on the day," Bess said, a small smile pushing up her lips.

"I'm glad, Bess," Jon said, and Bess could hear the honesty in his tone. "I mean, not for the bad days but that there are good ones again. I hate that I robbed you of so many good days."

Bess nodded. She knew her husband was sorry, and she believed it had been a one-time mistake. But that didn't change that it had happened. That he'd thrown away their wedding vows and had allowed another woman to become more important than her, even if it had been for just an afternoon. He'd forgotten her or stopped caring or whatever it was. And Bess wasn't sure she could forget that.

"Can I come home, Bess?" Jon asked softly, and Bess immediately shook her head no.

Jon's face fell, but he nodded as if he knew that was the answer that would be coming.

"I thought you might say that. So I started looking for a place in Seattle. My first choice would be to come home, but I acknowledge that I lost my right to my first choice."

Bess nodded. Yes he had.

"I'm sick of sleeping on my office couch. I need a place to rest my head. Even if it will never be home."

Bess wouldn't allow the poignant words to puncture her soul. Jon had given up his right to a home with her. "You've been staying at the office all this time?" Bess asked. She'd assumed he'd been at a hotel.

Jon nodded. "I was at a hotel for the first couple weeks, but that got old fast. I figured, why commute when my office has a comfy couch and there are plenty of good showers at the University gym. But that, too, has reached its expiration date."

That was why Jon hadn't come home to take more clothing with him. He didn't have the space. Bess' guest room was still littered with Jon's stuff—she'd closed the door when Stephen had come home—but now that he was getting his own place, Jon could take his stuff.

Bess wasn't sure how to respond to what Jon had said. He didn't deserve her sympathy, but saying, "*And you, sucker, are getting just what you deserve,*" didn't seem right either. So she settled on changing the subject.

"Did you walk up from the ferry?" Bess asked when she looked in the driveway and saw that Jon hadn't brought his car with him. It was more of a hassle to bring a car to the island than to ride a ferry as just a passenger.

"I had a car service pick me up from the dock," Jon said. "Is this your polite way of asking me to get out of here?"

Bess shrugged. "You came to see Stephen."

"I came to see both of you," Jon said.

Bess felt her heart ache. But it wasn't what she wanted to feel, so she pushed the feeling aside. She wanted to be done hurting over Jon. But wanting it and it happening were two very different things. She needed to make a decision. Allow herself and her heart to move on. Give some closure to her poor children. But she knew if she made a decision that night, she'd be rushing into things. She wasn't ready to press forward in one direction or another definitively yet. Taking Jon back would be the beginning of a whole new path, but divorce, well ... was it what they needed instead? She'd been unable to forgive Jon as of yet, but could that change? Could trust be rebuilt?

But right now Jon couldn't be here. Not now. Maybe not ever. And Jon needed to know that.

"I think you should go, Jon," Bess said.

Jon met her eyes, the sorrow easy to read. "I'm sorry, Bess," he whispered.

Bess believed him. She just didn't know if that was enough. "Good night, Jon," Bess said as she pushed off the railing and started for her front door.

"Good night, Bess," Jon said, his voice full of longing.

Bess kept on going and didn't stop until the front door was firmly closed behind her.

"Is he gone?" Stephen asked as he poked his head out of the hallway.

"He is."

"I'm sorry that you had to see him," Stephen said before walking back to his room.

Bess wished it was that black and white for her. She was sorry she had to see Jon as well, but she was also glad to have had communication with the person she'd shared everything with for thirty years. The confusion began to feel overwhelming. This was why people weren't meant to love and hate a single person at a given time. This was why her decision was full of gray and felt so impossible to make.

But Bess knew one thing. She couldn't live in this state of limbo forever. One day, soon, she'd have to make a choice. And that thought scared her to her very core.

TEN

DEB JUMPED out of bed the next morning, ready to take Rich down. She immediately called Doug, the attorney she'd recommended to Bess, and got his advice on what to do. Deb went through the money and assets they shared and calculated what her half would be. By the time her daughter got home from her slumber party, Deb was sure she looked like a crazy woman. But she was a crazy woman with a plan.

"Mom?" Bailee asked when she came into Deb's room and found that Deb was still in her pajamas and still in bed. Which wasn't unheard of for Deb, but it definitely wasn't a common occurrence.

"It's three pm," Bailee said, and Deb nodded from where she sat behind her laptop. It was incredible what could get done on the internet these days. Deb was getting her payback all while never leaving the comfort of her bed.

Bailee gave her a weird look before continuing down the hall to her own bedroom.

Deb's phone rang and she jumped to answer it, knowing it was probably her attorney.

"When do you want this petition for divorce served?" Doug asked after a formal greeting.

"As soon as possible." Deb wanted to be done with Rich and have him out of her life forever.

"Got it," he said with little emotion.

Deb understood that he did this on a daily basis, but she wanted someone else to feel the indescribable urge to ruin Rich that she did.

"We've talked about most of your assets and I've gotten your most recent emails, but what do you want to do about custody? Your daughter is still a minor, correct?"

Deb sat up straighter, feeling startled. She hadn't even thought about that because why should anything change? It wasn't like Rich visited them very often, and Bailee wasn't going to move to London. There was no way.

Deb explained as much to her lawyer, and he gave her a *hmmm*. Deb didn't like that *hmmm*.

"What do you mean by that?" Deb asked.

"This arrangement you have is a marital agreement. I have to warn you that when divorce comes into play, most of the time marital agreements go out the window," Doug said.

Deb felt sick to her stomach. She couldn't lose her daughter. But she also couldn't stay married to Rich.

"I'll put in the petition that you want full custody. But Deb," he paused, "you're going to have to be ready to fight for that one in court. Most people aren't willing to give up any form of custody easily."

Deb heard the warning, but she didn't care. She was ready to fight. Hell, she wanted a fight.

"Rich can bring it. He knows I never lose a fight," Deb growled.

Doug cleared his throat, probably grateful he'd never gone past the few dates he'd had with Deb many years before. Good.

She wanted to strike fear into the heart of every man, especially Rich.

"I think all that leaves is the reason for your petition for divorce," her attorney said.

"Let's see. Is the fact that he's a lying cheat who is living with his mistress while forgetting he has a family sufficient?" Deb asked.

"I'm not sure we have enough room for all of that on the petition, so let's go with adultery," Doug said in his no-nonsense voice.

Deb knew that was why he was good at his job, but come on. Couldn't he bash Rich for just a second? "Fine," she said, even though that word didn't come close to covering all that was pushing her to get this divorce.

"I'll talk to you again soon. And as a friend, can I give you a word of advice?" Doug asked.

Deb didn't need a friend who wanted to give advice. She needed a friend who was willing to slash Rich's tires. "What?" she asked, sounding as annoyed as she felt.

"Try to find some peace, Deb. This anger isn't hurting him," Doug said before hanging up.

Deb tossed her phone across her bed. Stupid man.

"Mom." Deb looked up to see Bailee in her bedroom doorway, and her heart sank. Why was she there? She wasn't supposed to witness any of this. Her daughter usually went straight to her room, closed her door and put in ear phones. Deb had just assumed ...

Crap. What had she heard?

"Who was that?" Bailee asked as she pointed to the phone.

"Um." Deb had been ready for every part of this divorce except her children. What was she supposed to do to save them? Her anger was her armor, but what did they have? She needed to arm them for battle as well.

"Were you talking about Dad?" Bailee asked.

Deb knew she had to tell her daughter the truth. She got out of bed and walked to Bailee, careful to keep eye contact the whole time. She wanted her to know that no matter what was coming next, Deb would always be there for her.

Only when Deb was right in front of her sweet girl did she say, "Yes. Your dad and I are getting a divorce, Bailee."

And Deb stood ready to catch her daughter as Bailee flung herself into Deb's arms.

ELEVEN

OLIVIA TOYED with her long blonde hair as she stared in the mirror at her gaunt face. She needed to start eating more, but she still wasn't hungry. It hadn't helped that her old neighbor had texted her a few days before that Bart's home was once again being resided in. By his latest mistress. Who was pregnant.

Olivia had fallen apart one more time, crying, aching, and pitying herself. But this time, she began to pick up the pieces faster than before. Her daughters needed a strong mother. Besides, the news shouldn't have surprised her. Bart needed a woman in his life, even if he wasn't going to love and cherish her. He just needed the role filled. Olivia wondered if that was why he'd been drinking so much at the reunion. Had he just found out his mistress was pregnant? And why had it been so easy to see Olivia and their girls go? He had another woman to fill her place, one with a child on the way. A ready-made family. And as much as the thought that they could all be replaced so easily tore her apart, Olivia knew her hurting would do nothing to change the situation. She had to push forward. She had to move on.

Thankfully, in the last couple of months she'd been speaking to an excellent therapist who'd given her coping techniques. And her therapist's insight had taught Olivia to see her harmful behavior and stop it nearly immediately. It made her stronger than she'd ever been. But even though Olivia was ready to be strong for herself and especially her girls, she still didn't have much of an appetite. Her mother had pointed out the night before that her nine-year-old daughter out-ate her, and Olivia knew even more had to change.

Bart had always loved Olivia's long blonde hair. She would go as far as to guess that his new woman in his home had long blonde hair too. He'd also demanded that Olivia be Botoxed, manicured, pedicured, waxed, facialed, and anything else he could find to help her appearance stay up to par. Olivia had quit all of those things as soon as she'd left Bart's home, but for some reason the blonde had stayed. Olivia looked at the pallor of her skin and was done with it.

She glanced at the time on her phone and saw that she had a few hours before she had to pick up her girls. Would Gen be too busy to fit her in right now? Olivia needed the change done today.

Olivia dialed the salon's number and asked the receptionist for Gen. She told Olivia that Gen was busy but would call her back when she could. Olivia set down the phone, feeling disappointed. The sudden urge to change her hair was so strong, she couldn't let it go. Dare she go with a box color? Gen would kill her.

Her phone rang a minute later, and Olivia jumped to answer it after seeing the incoming number belonged to Gen's cellphone.

"Gen?" she said into her phone.

"Hey, Olivia. Is everything okay?" Gen asked.

"Yes. No. Kind of. Um, maybe that was a hard question," Olivia said.

Gen laughed. "Let's go with something easier. Do you need anything?"

"How much would you hate me if I said I needed a color? Today?"

"I wouldn't hate you at all. I'd say come in right now."

"Really?" Olivia asked, her voice going high in disbelief. "But you're always booked out for months."

"I can always squeeze in a friend. I've got you, Olivia," Gen said kindly.

Olivia couldn't help the smile that spread over her face. Friend. She really needed to hear that. Olivia hadn't had one of those in so long, thanks to her messy and complicated world.

Thinking about her complicated life was all that Olivia needed to jump on Gen's offer of help. Olivia was used to doing it all on her own, a favor could always come back to bite her in the behind, but she was learning to let that fear go. Good people offering favors didn't come with strings. She needed to remember that.

"I'll be over in ten minutes," Olivia said to Gen, even though the drive alone would take her at least that long. But she was prepared to speed in order to get this mop on her head looking like the woman she wanted to be, not Bart's dream girl.

The drive into town took Olivia eight minutes, and she nearly ran into the salon from her parking spot on the drive.

"I'm here to see Gen," Olivia said to the receptionist, Kate, as the woman behind the desk pulled up Gen's schedule on her computer. Olivia had been a frequent enough customer that Kate knew her on sight.

"Oh, Olivia, I'm sorry but—"

"That's okay, Kate," Gen said as she came out from the main portion of the salon into the reception area. "I told Olivia I'd squeeze her in. Do you mind offering Mrs. Smith a drink when she gets here and bringing her back to me? I don't think I'll have time to come out to greet her."

"Sure thing, Gen," Kate said with a smile to Olivia and then Gen before turning her attention back to her computer screen.

"What do you feel like drinking?" Gen asked Olivia as she walked her back to her station.

"A bottle of water would be great," Olivia said as Gen settled Olivia into her seat and put a cape around her.

"Are you sure? We've got lattes, cappuccinos, and champagne," Gen offered.

Olivia shook her head.

"Or maybe just a diet coke?" Gen added.

"I'm really okay with water," Olivia said, giving Gen a soft smile before catching her own reflection in the mirror. She really needed to get rid of this blonde. She hated that every time she looked in the mirror, she saw the woman Bart had wanted her to be. In just a few hours, all of this blonde would be gone.

After Olivia was settled, Gen left to go to the back of the salon for a few seconds before reappearing. "Here ya go," Gen said, giving Olivia the bottle of water she had asked for and then playing with Olivia's hair, gently pulling the strands between her fingers.

"Thanks," Olivia said at the same time Gen said, "So what are you thinking you want to do?"

Need was the more appropriate word for what Olivia was doing—she was so far beyond *wanting* her long, blonde mane gone—but she figured saying that was a little too much insight into her crazy brain.

"I want to go shorter. Maybe shoulder length," Olivia said, and Gen grinned. Olivia would get to her ideas about hair color after Gen washed her hair. After the wash and before the final cut was the time Gen typically asked her about color. Before that day it had almost always been the same. Blonde or blonder. Olivia's heart ramped up in anticipation. If Gen was this smiley about Olivia going short, she could only imagine her reaction to Olivia going red.

"That's a whole lot shorter, but it will look amazing on you. A woman as gorgeous as you doesn't need all of this hair," Gen said as she continued to play with Olivia's hair.

Olivia shook her head in response to Gen because right now, the last thing she felt was gorgeous. However, after this cut and color, Olivia hoped she would at least feel a lot more like herself, not the woman she'd pretended to be for so many years.

"So let's get started," Gen said as she pulled out a pair of scissors and began to do a rough cut of Olivia's dry hair.

"You know as well as I do that conversation is usually a big part of this whole hair cutting process." Gen paused to grin at Olivia in the mirror, and Olivia returned a grin. "But before we start to talk, I figure we need to get one thing straight. I'm not going to ask about anything to do with what's going on in your life because I don't want to pry. But I don't want you to take that as disinterest. You talk about anything you want to talk about, Olivia," Gen said earnestly as she finished cutting the length off and motioned for Olivia to stand before leading her back to the hair washing station.

Olivia shot Gen a grateful smile as they walked. Then she noticed that Gen was keeping her away from the other women in the salon as if she were protecting Olivia from their attention, and Olivia couldn't be more appreciative. Gen was proving to be the best kind of friend.

Olivia stayed silent during the blissful hair washing and head massage session and then followed Gen back to her station. As she sat back in Gen's chair, a drop of water fell from the towel her hair was wrapped in and down her forehead. Olivia swiped at the drop of water as Gen undid Olivia's towel hair turban.

"Do you want your cut to be blunt on the edges?" Gen asked.

Old Olivia would have jumped at the suggestion. The severe cut would have been the only way Olivia would have done a shorter cut a few months before. But today Olivia wanted everything about her new look to be the opposite of what Bart would have liked, and she knew he hated layers that framed her face.

"I think I want some layers," Olivia said, and Gen grinned again.

"I'm going to adore this new look," Gen said when Olivia drew in a deep breath.

"And I want to go red."

Gen's eyes went wide for a split second before she schooled her features, just leaving behind a huge smile. It was fun to see her surprise, even through her professional exterior.

"More like your natural color," Gen said as she met Olivia's eyes.

Olivia nodded. She'd been covering her original rich brown color enriched by lots of red highlights with blonde hair dye since she was sixteen. Not surprisingly, about the same time she'd started dating Bart.

"But even redder," Olivia said.

Gen nodded. "I can do that," she said as she walked away to a nearby table and came back with a few pictures.

"Are you thinking red like this or like this?" Gen asked as she showed the pictures to Olivia.

Olivia glanced through the pictures and landed on the photo of Emma Stone.

"Exactly what I was hoping," Gen said when she noticed where Olivia's eyes had gone. "You know you kind of look like her."

Olivia couldn't see it as she stared at her reflection once again. The woman who looked back at her appeared to be worn out and every bit her thirty-eight years. The woman in the photo was bright, young, and vibrant. Things Olivia couldn't even remember being.

Gen combed out Olivia's wet hair and then took her scissors out. Gen had already gotten rid of lots of the length when Olivia's hair had been dry, but now she took her time as she created Olivia's new style.

"I look tired," Olivia said, more to her reflection than to Gen.

Gen shook her head. "You look amazing. You always have, and that was before you had this new light in your eyes."

New light? What was Gen seeing that Olivia was missing?

"What are you talking about?" Olivia asked as she raised an eyebrow, meeting Gen's eyes through the mirror.

"I know what you're going through is rough. No, I take that back. I don't *know* anything. But I can imagine how rough it must be. Even with all of that, you look happier, Liv."

Olivia looked from Gen's reflection to her own. Was she happier? She knew she felt lighter because she no longer had Bart's expectations breathing down her neck. But even with that relief, she still missed the excitement she used to feel every Friday evening, knowing Bart would be coming back to her. And part of her knew it was sick that she had been so thrilled even though she knew she only owned a portion of her husband's heart. But because it was all that she'd known for so long, she'd come to accept it. She had so desperately wanted Bart to love her that she'd been willing to take whatever he'd give her. So was she happier now? Not having to just accept what Bart was willing to give? She could be. She wasn't sure of much these days.

Olivia focused on the mirror and saw that there was no one behind her. Her guess was that Gen had left to go mix up some color while Olivia had been deep in her thoughts. And Olivia would have been pleased to continue alone with her thoughts, but when she looked up in the mirror, she saw one of the people she'd been working hard to avoid since leaving Bart making a beeline right for her. Olivia knew luck wasn't on her side. She wished she'd had the foresight to have a magazine or even her phone in her hands, but she was completely available when Whitney Barker ambushed her.

"I am so sorry, Olivia. You must feel terrible about yourself," Whitney said in her nasally tone as she looked Olivia up and down, telling Olivia that not only should she feel terrible about herself, she looked terrible as well.

Olivia knew Whitney and her reputation well since, like Olivia, Whitney had lived on the island for her whole life and they'd only been a year apart in school. Whitney stood beside her and then went so far as to place a hand on Olivia's arm in what must have been an attempt at condolence. But Olivia could see from Whitney's eyes that she was hiding a smile behind her exaggerated frown.

"Thank you, Whitney," Olivia said, trying to sound gracious instead of hurt before looking away from the woman. Olivia knew better than to show Whitney that she was getting under Olivia's skin.

Beautiful Whitney hadn't been Olivia's friend in high school or since, but not for Whitney's lack of trying. Olivia had always tried to keep a wide berth of the woman because she'd hated the way Whitney was the center of too much of the drama that happened on the island. Anyone who was close to Whitney seemed to be sucked into the vortex of her never-ending crises.

But Whitney had been unhappy, to say the least, when Olivia hadn't joined her circle of friends. She'd started rumors that Olivia thought she was too good for the rest of them and that was the reason Olivia wouldn't join them for their bookless and very gossip-filled book clubs and Friday brunches. Olivia hadn't appreciated the rumors but figured they were better than giving in to Whitney. However, she could only imagine the satisfaction Whitney had gotten with Olivia's fall from grace.

But apparently Whitney wasn't done rubbing salt in Olivia's wound because she stayed beside her as she said, "I mean, for Bart to cheat on you is one thing. But now moving his mistress into your house? Don't worry, I already hate her. She'll have a tough time making any friends on this island." Whitney continued to pat Olivia's arm, and Olivia suddenly felt light-headed. She realized she'd been holding her breath, waiting for Whitney's bombshell to drop. And there it was.

Olivia had known Bart had moved his mistress to the island, but she hadn't even thought about the fact that the woman would now be running in her same circles. The island was too small for her not to. She'd be making friends on the island. She was here full-time, unlike Bart. Olivia had been too preoccupied trying to ignore that Bart had replaced her so easily to think about the day to day repercussions of his actions. This woman's life would be here.

Olivia drew in a deep breath and tried to keep her expression neutral. Whitney's shrewd gaze was taking in every detail about Olivia. Yes, this was a rude awakening, but nothing had really changed. Bart's mistress had been here for a while. So far, Olivia hadn't run into her. Hopefully that blessing could continue until Olivia was in a head and heart space to see the woman who had taken her place.

And Olivia was already stronger than she had been, right? She could share an island with Bart's new girlfriend, even if she didn't want to. Besides, Olivia was grateful to be out from under Bart's thumb. This new hair color proved it. If anything, Olivia should feel badly for the woman taking her place.

"Don't keep from getting to know her on my account," Olivia

said after taking in air that helped to normalize her breathing again. She knew Whitney had wanted Olivia to start bashing her replacement, but she was glad she'd taken a moment to really think about things before saying anything. Even if she'd never be best friends with the woman, she should at least try to remain cordial, if only for the sake of her girls.

Whoever this woman was, she wasn't to blame for the dissolution of Olivia's marriage to Bart. If Olivia really thought about it, Olivia hadn't ever had much of a marriage. It was coming to terms with that that was so hard. Sure, Bart's mistress was a bruise to her ego, but his years of cheating coming to light had obliterated any kind of pride Olivia had. The bruise wasn't much after the beating Olivia had already endured.

"Well, it isn't just for you. None of us want to associate with a woman who is so delighted to wreck a home. Such a perfect home, at that," Whitney said.

Olivia swore there was quite a bit of sarcasm behind the word "perfect." Even though Whitney had meant for her sarcasm to be cruel, Olivia couldn't blame Whitney for her skepticism. Olivia's life had been so far from the perfect facade that she'd tried to create. Now that that facade had been blown to smithereens, who could blame a woman like Whitney from poking at the remaining embers.

But she did have to admit that Whitney being upset about Bart's mistress breaking up Olivia's family was definitely the pot calling the kettle black if the island's gossip held any truth. Apparently Whitney had done plenty of her own home wrecking after being left by her own husband a few years before. But Olivia wasn't about to judge anyone. Not even Whitney Barker. One thing she'd learned over the last few months was no one knew what anyone else was going through.

"Oh, but in great news, I heard Dean is home for good again," Whitney said, thankfully changing the subject.

Olivia had to admit her heart sped up a bit at hearing Dean's name. Which was ridiculous because Dean was a friend, at most. Did their quick run-in at the park warrant enough of a reunion to allow Olivia to call Dean a friend again? Because in the last many years, they hadn't even been that.

Olivia stayed quiet that she already knew Dean had moved home because she'd spoken to the man himself. She could only imagine Whitney's reaction to Olivia having had a conversation with Dean and opted for a simple, "That's nice."

Finally Gen came out of the color room, and her eyes went wide when she saw who had cornered Olivia. She looked from Whitney to the room at large, probably looking for Whitney's stylist.

"Didn't Dean buy a home close to your sister?" Whitney asked Gen when she came to her spot behind Olivia.

Gen nodded but didn't smile. Olivia imagined Gen wasn't a big fan of a woman like Whitney Barker. But considering Whitney's mane was full of extensions and lots of other expensive procedures, Gen had to bite her tongue.

"He was always so hot, but have you seen him recently? He blows handsome high school Dean out of the water," Whitney said.

Olivia watched as Gen made eye contact with another stylist who walked out of the color room just then, and soon that woman was at Whitney's side.

"I'm ready for you whenever you are, Whit," the stylist said.

Whitney smiled. "I've got to go, but it was great talking to you, Olivia. I've missed seeing you around. Please don't hide away because ..." Whitney let her voice trail off as she frowned.

Gen looked between Whitney's stylist and Whitney, silently urging the former to get a move on.

"You too, Whitney," Olivia said as the woman finally walked away.

"I'm sorry that I left you alone. Had I any idea ..." Gen whispered.

Olivia shook her head, giving Gen a smile through the mirror. The encounter with Whitney hadn't been pleasant, but it was over. Besides, it wasn't Gen's job to protect her.

"It was fine," Olivia said.

Gen met Olivia's eyes. "You, my dear, are a lot kinder than I am. Whitney Barker needs to come with a warning label," Gen whispered as the woman in question took a seat on the other side of the salon.

Olivia giggled, feeling much better now that Whitney was gone. Even though she had survived Whitney, that didn't mean Olivia wanted to continue the conversation.

"She tends to hit below the belt. But that doesn't mean what she says isn't the truth," Olivia said.

Gen shook her head. "She takes a small part of the truth and twists it in an effort to make everyone else look bad. She hired Levi to work on her house recently, and I swear if she hits on him one more time ..." Gen brought her color brush away from Olivia's hair and to her side, knowing not to color while agitated.

"I'm sorry, Gen," Olivia said, meeting Gen's eyes in the mirror.

Gen shrugged before going back to Olivia's hair. "I guess it's my fault for marrying such a hot guy."

Olivia laughed. "If that's your worst sin, you sure are living some fun consequences," Olivia responded. Then she added, "At least Levi is being honest with you and not jumping at the bait."

What would it be like to have a husband who honored fidelity?

Gen covered a piece of Olivia's hair with foil before pausing in her work. "How are the girls doing?" Gen asked.

Olivia smiled, thinking about the major bright spot in her

life. "Amazing. Somehow the gossip hasn't hit the elementary school scene, for which I am grateful to our little island. Bart was so absent from their lives that living with my parents and not seeing their father is just one grand adventure for them. It's crazy how resilient they really are."

"Thus the saying," Gen responded as she painted dye onto Olivia's hair.

Olivia nodded. "But part of me kind of hates that they aren't even missing him. What kind of man did I choose for my girls? I remember being crushed when my dad went on a week-long business trip. My girls haven't even asked about Bart, and it's been months."

Gen focused on her work, but by the look on her face, Olivia could tell she was also thinking about what Olivia had said.

"You chose this guy when you were sixteen. I think you should give yourself a break," Gen said.

Olivia shook her head. "I chose him again when I was seventeen, eighteen, and every year after that," Olivia said, ashamed that the kind of father Bart would be hadn't even occurred to her until she'd held the pregnancy stick that read positive for the very first time.

"You should still give yourself a break," Gen said kindly, and Olivia had to smile at her friend's sweetness. "And maybe lay a little of this blame on Bart. He's the one choosing to be this man."

Olivia laughed at Gen's tone of voice and the sassy tilt of her head, but when she replayed the words in her head, her laughing ceased. Why wasn't she blaming Bart?

Gen watched as Olivia took in her words and then spoke again as if she knew Olivia needed a change of subject. Which she did. "Have you heard about Bess' food truck?" Gen asked.

Olivia nodded. "It's the talk of the island. Seriously, your sister is incredible, and her food is even better," Olivia said.

"Honestly, the food Bess has brought over has been one of the greatest perks about living with my parents again."

Gen laughed. "Isn't it good? We've been telling her that for years. I'm so glad she's finally acting on it. Not that I'm glad about the reason that pushed her to do it."

Olivia nodded. Bess had overcome so much in such a short time. Instead of being crushed and allowing herself to be tromped on by the Whitney Barkers of the world, Bess was rebuilding her life and starting a food truck. Olivia wanted that to be her. Her parents had been amazing and supportive, telling her to take all the time she needed to figure things out. But she knew everyone was waiting to see what Olivia's next move would be, and so far, she had none. Why couldn't she be more like Bess?

Gen secured the last foil in Olivia's hair as Olivia's phone rang. She took the ringing device out of her purse. The number that stared back at her wasn't a friendly one, but she had to take the call anyway.

"It's my lawyer," Olivia said, and Gen took a step back from Olivia's hair. "I need to take it."

She'd been waiting for this call for months. She'd heard nothing from the man, and considering Bart had texted him the day that Olivia had moved out, it was about time he'd gotten around to talking to her.

"Of course. Do you want to use my office for some privacy?" Gen asked, and Olivia nodded gratefully. The last thing she needed was for Whitney Barker to overhear her call with her attorney.

"Hello?" Olivia answered as she scurried back to Gen's office and then closed the door behind her.

"Olivia, I'm glad I caught you. I just got off the phone with Bart and wanted to review the terms for the dissolution of your marriage," the lawyer said. Olivia's stomach clenched at the smooth tone in which he said, *"Dissolution of your marriage."* As if it were easy for them to tear apart what had been together for years.

"Yes," Olivia said because she lacked any better words.

"Bart wants to keep the home," the man said.

Olivia wasn't surprised considering he'd already moved his mistress into the house. But Olivia didn't want it. To her, every space in that home would always be a part of Bart. She needed to move on, so she was content to see it go.

"And most of his assets. He's happy for you to keep the car that you drive, and he'll pay you a generous monthly alimony along with child support for your daughters."

Wait, Bart was keeping everything and giving Olivia an allowance? That's what it sounded like to her. She knew most of what they owned was in Bart's name, including her car, so is this what her life had come to? She'd supported Bart in every way that she could, but because he was the one who'd made all of the money, it was now all his?

"I can draw up legal documents to reflect the agreement, and we should have this thing tied up with a neat bow in a couple of weeks," the attorney continued without needing Olivia to say a word. Why would he? He and Bart had already figured this all out.

"Thank you for your time, Olivia. Goodbye." The attorney hung up, and Olivia stared at her phone, wondering what had just happened.

She opened the door to Gen's office and walked back into the salon, knowing she should be feeling or thinking more. But her brain felt like the fog she'd taken months to clear was back, and it had now extended to her soul.

"Are you okay, Olivia?" Gen asked as Olivia walked back to Gen's station.

Olivia nodded but then stopped. Was she okay?

Gen helped Olivia to sit back down in front of the mirror, and it was then that Olivia noticed how pale her countenance was. She knew Gen wouldn't push her to talk about anything, but Olivia realized she could use a friend and sounding board right about now.

"That was our attorney. We are on what he says will be a quick path to divorce," Olivia said quietly.

Gen put up her hand. "*Our* attorney?" she asked.

Olivia nodded.

"You are sharing a divorce attorney with your soon to be ex?" Gen asked, her eyes wide.

Olivia nodded again. "I just figured this would cause less mess. The last thing I need is some big, drawn out divorce," Olivia said, still trying to rid herself of the stupid fog. Why wouldn't it stay away?

"I get that," Gen said slowly as if she didn't quite get it but was trying to understand anyway. "Is he someone you and Bart found together?"

Olivia shook her head. "He's been Bart's attorney for years. Bart mentioned it would be good to have someone who knew our situation instead of bringing in a stranger."

"Olivia, this man works for your husband. Not you," Gen said, helping Olivia out of her chair so that she could walk to one of the hair processors.

"He works for both of us," Olivia said, but Gen's words had put some doubt in her mind.

Gen got called away by Kate to do something, and while she was gone, Olivia had plenty of time to think. She'd assumed since the divorce was for both of them, their attorney would advocate for both of them. But was that not the case? Considering how little she was going to be leaving the marriage with, maybe it wasn't. She'd seen divorces on TV and in the movies, but in her real life, no one had had to cross that bridge. Olivia had just wanted to throw all of this mess at someone else and have them take care of it, but Gen was right. How could a man who worked for her husband have her best interest at heart?

"Does he really work for *both* of you?" Gen asked when she came back, checking the foils on Olivia's head. "This is done," Gen declared, leading Olivia back to the sinks.

Could a man employed by Bart feel equal alliance to them both? Olivia felt stupid at her lack of foresight but was humble enough to know she needed Gen's help. As Gen washed her hair, Olivia quietly explained the terms of her divorce to Gen. Fortunately, Whitney had left the salon by this point, but who knew what other ears would be trying to listen. By the immediate scowl on Gen's face, Olivia figured she must be getting the short end of the stick. It had been so easy to let Bart take care of this, the way he'd taken care of everything else in their life. However, she had to remember she and Bart were on opposing sides; her interests weren't his interests.

"Olivia, those are the most ridiculous terms to a divorce that I've ever heard. You know that you deserve more than that, don't you?" Gen said as Olivia sat back at Gen's station so that Gen could put the final touches on Olivia's haircut.

"Maybe? But Bart is the one who worked...."

"You raised your children, stood by his side and loved him," Gen said as she snipped away at the now red locks. But even as she listed what Olivia had done in their shared home, it didn't seem like enough. She hadn't cooked and cleaned. They had Patty and their maids for that. Sure, she felt like she'd been busy every day of their entire marriage, but what did she have to show for it? Bart's daily work had built him a multi-million dollar company.

"You need to hire your own attorney," Gen said, putting her shears down and lifting her blow dryer to finish the job.

Olivia was about to express her doubts, but the sound of the blow dryer cut her off, giving her more time to think. Maybe she should look into the guy her brother had recommended? Why was she trusting Bart with this when she knew she hadn't been able to trust Bart with her heart for years. She figured he would have no trouble looking out for their financial interests because he always had before. But this was really different, wasn't it?

Man, she'd been a fool again. And she wasn't a stupid woman. Although her entire marriage and now her divorce had plenty of evidence to the contrary. But she had promised she would stop beating herself up. She'd been brought to see the light in another part of her life, and for that she should be grateful, not leading the charge in tearing herself down.

"Olivia." Gen interrupted her thoughts as the blow dryer turned off. "You are a capable and strong woman. I have seen you put together charity dinners that rivaled royal events with basically just your two hands. You raised two amazing little girls practically on your own. Know your worth, Olivia. Do you need help in finding an attorney?"

Olivia shook her head, remembering her brother.

"Dax knows a guy," Olivia said, and Gen grinned.

"Of course he does. Your family must be chomping at the bit to help you," Gen said.

Olivia nodded. They had been. But Olivia had pushed them away. Not as much as she had while married, but she was yet to let anyone fully into her mess of a world because she was ashamed. Her family had no idea she was sharing an attorney with Bart—Olivia always changed the subject when they tried to broach the topic—and she realized if her family knew the truth, they'd be as appalled as Gen. Look where that had gotten her. If she hadn't opened up to Gen, she might have settled with Bart and gotten way less than she deserved out of her years of struggle. Olivia was trying to change and not keep herself closed off from the world, but all of that was coming slowly. However, she realized her attempt to keep people from seeing her too well was only hurting herself.

No more.

Gen was a brilliant friend, and Olivia smiled up at the woman who she'd needed in more ways than one that day.

Gen returned her smile and held a mirror up to Olivia so that she could take in the whole look from the back and the front. Olivia immediately fell in love.

"What do you think?" Gen asked.

"It's incredible," Olivia said.

Gen wasn't just a brilliant friend, she was also a genius with hair. Olivia's hair not only felt better and lighter, but she looked younger and more refreshed than she had in years. She felt like a brand new person, exactly what she'd needed.

As Olivia spun in her chair, she found herself thinking Gen was right. Olivia needed to know her worth. She might not know it yet, but she hoped to one day.

TWELVE

BESS PUSHED the vacuum one last time across the carpet, finishing the cleaning of her entire house. She'd been avoiding house cleaning ever since she began to run with the idea of the food truck, but now that she was having her newest employee over, she decided it was time to get things in much better shape.

Gen had called Bess as soon as Olivia had left her salon with her new red hair, which the island gossips were loving. Gen explained Olivia's situation to Bess, detailing how Bart's attorney had taken advantage of Olivia. Then Gen asked Bess what her attorney had done for her to make sure the same wouldn't happen to Bess. Gen was pleased to hear Bess' attorney was much more adept than Olivia's had been.

Gen still thought it was too quick for Bess to be taking legal measures against her husband, but with Deb on the other end of the spectrum pushing Bess to go through with her divorce as fast as Deb was pushing hers, Gen felt good about the Bess' happy medium. She'd talked to Doug, the attorney Deb had recommended, to get advice but so far wasn't moving forward with anything.

Gen was trying to be supportive, but Bess knew that Gen

loved Jon. He'd been a part of almost her whole life and was definitely more of a brother than a brother-in-law to her.

But Bess had to do what was right for her. After hours and hours of soul searching during long walks on the beach, this was it. She needed to move forward in the ways that she felt comfortable. That meant starting the food truck and that meant keeping her mind open to divorcing a man she wasn't sure she would ever be able to trust again. She'd given him every part of her, and he'd betrayed her. He couldn't take that back.

After the attorney talk was settled, Bess went on to share with Gen the headaches she was facing with starting her new business. If anyone knew what it was like to grow something from the ground up, it was Gen. Her salon had begun as a one-woman shop in her home and was now a twenty-person operation on the busiest street in town.

When Bess talked about how hard it was going to be to manage all of the food, food prep, and shopping, as well as the business side of things, Gen gasped.

"I know what you should do," Gen said.

Bess wasn't sure what was going to come out of Gen's mouth.

"Hire Olivia. I remember her telling me she did her husband's bookkeeping when he first started. That's exactly the kind of experience you need. And heaven knows she needs a way to move forward," Gen said.

Bess immediately latched onto the idea. Olivia was smart; she knew that from being her teacher. And even though Bess might've wanted someone with a little more experience, she liked that she and Olivia would be learning together as they went. And it wasn't like Bess had a ton of money to burn. She had a feeling Olivia would come much cheaper than someone with years of experience.

So she called Olivia, offered her the job, and now Olivia and

Gen were coming over today to talk specifics. Olivia and Bess both figured they could use Gen's experience.

Bess' front door opened and closed—Bess assumed Gen had arrived— as Bess made her way into the kitchen to check on the lasagna she had bubbling in the oven. They'd decided to make this a working lunch, and she hoped what she couldn't offer to pay Olivia, she could make up for in delicious food.

"Is that for me?" Deb asked, startling Bess and causing her to slam the oven shut instead of gently closing it.

"Hello to you too, Deb," Bess said.

Deb waved her comment away. "So is it?" Deb asked. "Because my day has been terrible, but I'm sure a load of cheese and carbs could go a long way in fixing it."

"Rich?" Bess asked.

"Who else?" Deb responded before continuing. "So about that lasagna?"

"It's for Gen and my new employee," Bess said proudly.

"Seriously? That's fantastic, Bess," Deb said happily, all of her earlier agitation either gone or hidden well before she looked longingly at the lasagna. "But the three of you can't possibly finish that whole thing."

"It's still got a few minutes to cook, but there's a piece in there just for you," Bess said.

Deb sat down on a stool at the counter with a satisfied smile on her face.

"So back to you. Do you want to talk about it?" Bess asked. She didn't want Deb's foul mood to return, but her friend needed her.

"Talk about what a selfish bastard my ex is? Sure. This was supposed to be a simple parting of our assets and our lives, considering we've kept our finances separate from the beginning. We had a small amount of funds in combined accounts and our only combined purchases were the house here and our apartment from our early years of marriage in New York that we've kept as a rental. We agreed that I would keep this house and he'd get the apartment. It's what made sense because my life is here. But I just got word from Rich that he and his snake of an attorney got the apartment appraised, and it's worth a hundred thousand less than the house here. Rich had the nerve to tell me that he wants me to pay him that hundred thousand dollars. I don't have that kind of money just lying around to give my ex in order to get him off my back. So I told him that we can go to court and I was sure a judge wouldn't be very impressed with the fact that he's been living with his mistress for the last six months of our marriage. He said the judge would probably be fine with that when he heard I wouldn't move with him to London and was unsupportive of his career. Then I told him to shove it and hung up on him."

"That probably went over well," Bess said as she checked on the lasagna again. Deb might be mad now, but if Bess burned the lasagna ... well, Bess wouldn't want to be in the same room as her friend if that happened.

"He tried to call back, but I ignored his calls. And now his stupid attorney emailed saying Rich is going back on our custody agreement. He wants Bailee to come live with him for her last month of her senior year. He's willing to use our daughter as a pawn just to spite me. What kind of father would tear his daughter away from her life in the last month of her entire schooling just to get back at his ex?" Deb looked like she wanted to punch or throw something, so Bess moved the vase on the counter out of Deb's reach.

"He can't do that, can he?" Bess asked, her stomach in knots for her friend. Jon might have done the unthinkable to her, but he would never stoop to this. At least she hoped he wouldn't. He loved his children too much. And thankfully, her children were too old for a custody agreement. But she knew that hadn't kept others in their situation from using their children as pawns in their disagreements.

"My attorney says we can tie up the paperwork in court for long enough that it wouldn't be done before summer, thus ensuring Rich couldn't get his month. But the fact that he would say that? Use our sweet Bailee like that? Now he's in for a fight." Deb gritted her teeth.

Even though Bess was as little a fan of Rich as Deb was, she couldn't help but feel a little sorry for him. Deb had the creative mind of an artist but the bite of a pit bull. A creative way to be bitten in the behind was never something to look forward to.

But did Deb really want to fight?

"Are you sure a fight is the best idea?" Bess asked cautiously.

"He's the one who started it. But you know me well enough to know I'll be the one to end it."

Bess nodded, wanting to be supportive of her friend. But she couldn't help but wonder at what cost this would all come. She would have to be vigilant in her friendship with Deb in the coming months. She had a feeling her best friend would need her now more than ever. She looked from Deb to her home and wondered how they'd both gotten here. When they began their friendship with loving husbands by their sides over twenty years before, she would have never guessed this would be their future.

The doorbell rang, and Bess pulled out the lasagna before hurrying to answer the door. She wiped her hands on her apron before opening it.

"Olivia," Bess said as she held out her arms to hug the woman at her doorstep. It probably wasn't conventional boss/employee etiquette, but none of what was happening in Bess' life right now was conventional.

"Bess," Olivia said as she sank into Bess' hug. "Thank you for hiring me. I won't let you down."

Bess knew that. It was why she'd jumped at the opportunity

to have Olivia on her team. They both pulled away from the hug as Bess said, "Thank you for taking a job with a home cook armed only with a dream and an upcoming divorce."

Olivia laughed along with Bess as the sound of Gen's car coming up Bess' driveway caused them both to look at the direction of the sound.

"Hello, Olivia, Bess!" Gen called out from her car before getting out and walking toward Bess' front door.

"Good to see you, Gen," Olivia said as Bess smiled her greeting to her sister.

"Perfect timing," Bess said as she let the women into her home. "I'm just getting the lasagna out of the oven."

"You're going to feed me?" Olivia asked. "Best job ever," she said with a grin that Bess had to return.

The beautiful Olivia was looking miles better than when Bess had last seen her walking down her parents' driveway to check the mail a few weeks earlier. Her shorter, red hair suited her complexion and her dark green eyes, and it looked like she'd even been able to put on a few pounds after losing so many since moving out of the home she'd resided in all of her marriage.

"And here it is," Deb said grandly as she set the pan of lasagna on the dining room table Bess had set with her best china earlier that day—the stuff she only used for special occasions.

Bess smiled gratefully at her friend, knowing she was putting aside her own problems for the time being for Bess.

Bess turned to Olivia. "Should we start with food and then go into the logistics of the job?" Bess asked.

"Always start with food," Deb said, and the other women laughed as Bess served them all a piece of the cheesy delight.

Only after taking her first bite of lasagna did Bess pull out her business plan that she'd worked on for hours with Levi.

She was too excited to sit and eat when there was still so much to do. She passed the stack of papers to Olivia who studied them as she ate. Bess took a bite here and there but was much more focused on Olivia and the papers than she was on the lasagna.

"This looks fantastic. We all know I'm no expert in business —ten years out of the game will do that to you—but I do have a bachelor's degree in finance," Olivia said, sounding more confident in her abilities than she had even a few days before when Bess had offered her the job.

"You didn't tell me that," Bess said, feeling proud of her find. Or she guessed Olivia was Gen's find.

"Well, a degree in finance doesn't mean much when I only have about three years of work experience in the field over ten years ago."

"Hey, I'm not one to judge. I haven't worked in over twenty," Bess countered.

"No. You've both worked. And you've worked hard. You not only raised your kids, you managed your homes," Gen said as she looked at Olivia.

"I did," Olivia said, accepting the praise with a small smile.

"So no more putting down all that we have done in the last however many years," Gen said.

Bess nodded. Her sister was right.

"Well, the business plan looks amazing. I'm pretty sure I know which steps we should take next. I think I want to start a social media campaign for the truck. With how small the island is, word of mouth is the best marketing tool we can wield," Olivia said.

Bess loved that idea. But she was useless when it came to anything social media.

"Don't look so worried, Bess. That will be my job. I'll also look into hiring an accounting firm to get started on the stuff that's over my head. I'll take the books as far as I can and then get someone else to help me with the rest," Olivia said.

Bess felt her chest get lighter. She'd been feeling so overwhelmed by every task. It felt incredible for some of that weight to be gone.

"I love those ideas," Bess said. Then she looked to Gen.

"Sounds perfect to me too. I have a feeling Scratch Made by Bess will be seeing success sooner rather than later," Gen said.

"I'll drink to that," Deb said as she raised her water glass and then prompted the other women to do the same.

"To Scratch Made by Bess," Deb declared.

"To Scratch Made by Bess," the other women mimicked as they clinked their glasses together.

Bess couldn't help the huge grin on her face. This was really happening.

"Now back to the important stuff. I'm going in for a second piece of lasagna. Anyone else want one?" Deb asked as she spooned another serving onto her plate.

Olivia passed her plate forward, but Gen and Bess opted out. They'd both had more than their fill of Bess' rich food over the past couple of months with all of Bess' experimenting.

"Olivia. Can I say, single life looks good on you," Deb said as she passed Olivia's plate back.

Olivia smiled. "I have to say it feels good too. Well, that's a lie. It doesn't feel good all the time, but today it does," she said.

"Take that win, girl," Gen said. "Did you talk to your brother about an attorney yet?"

Olivia nodded. "And I already spoke to Mr. Johnson, the attorney. He said the deal Bart's attorney offered was atrocious."

"Atrocious. That's a big word for an attorney," Deb teased.

Olivia laughed.

"But he was speaking the truth. Atrocious is the only word adequate enough to describe what Bart was trying to do to you. I like Mr. Johnson already. Do you mind if I share what Bart's attorney offered?" Gen asked Olivia.

"By all means. I want people to know how much better a deal I'm going to secure for myself," Olivia said with a pump of her eyebrows.

Deb clapped. "Yes! That is what I like to hear."

Gen told the women what Bart's attorney had tried to give to Olivia, causing Deb to gasp. Even Bess felt shocked.

"You told the guy to shove that deal where the sun don't shine, right?" Deb asked.

Olivia giggled. "I guess I did do something like that after talking to Mr. Johnson."

"Good," Deb said before taking another bite of lasagna. "Men are the worst. I guess I have to keep my attorney, Doug, out of that statement because he's going to go to war with me. But the rest? Terrible."

"Hey. What about Levi?" Gen asked.

Deb shrugged. "You tell me?" Deb asked.

"He's amazing," Gen said firmly.

Gen was used to Deb's sometimes harsh ways, but she wasn't as forgiving of them as her sister. She could handle Deb as a friend, but Gen often wondered how Deb could be the one woman Bess chose to be her friend above all others, besides Gen.

"If you say so," Deb said. "But if you could all convince me to get Bess to finally pull the trigger on her divorce proceedings, that would be great. We know Jon is in the *worst* category."

"I talked to Doug, Deb. That's as far as I want to go for now," Bess said as she stood and began to gather the dirty plates before taking them to the kitchen sink. She then turned back to the table as she leaned against the counter.

"And Jon isn't the worst. He made a mistake," Gen said, furrowing her brow.

Deb cocked her head and set down her fork. "Now I'm second guessing your opinion on Levi because Jon definitely sucks," Deb said, a frown deeply etched onto her face.

Gen shook her head, her face adorned with a frown nearly as severe as Deb's. "You can't discount all of the good he's done because of one thing."

"If that one thing is cheating, yes I can," Deb said, raising her eyebrows.

Gen crossed her arms over her chest. "Maybe *you* can, but that doesn't mean that Bess should."

"But Bess should," Deb countered, and Gen narrowed her eyes.

"Do you want your sister to stay with a man who has no respect for her?" Deb asked.

"How do you know that's how Jon feels? Are you in his head?" Gen cocked her head.

"No. But I doubt Bess was when he cheated on her."

"Hey," Bess said, feeling Deb had gone too far. They both had. This was her life and her decision.

"I'm sorry, Bess," Deb said as she pushed her hair out of her face, looking sorrowfully at her friend. "I shouldn't have said that. But before we move on, I really need to say this."

Bess saw the fierce glint that had entered Deb's eyes and figured if Deb didn't say what she wanted to now, she would later. Might as well get it over with.

"Okay," Bess said cautiously.

"This truck. What if it's wildly successful? If you don't divorce Jon now, he has rights to half of it," Deb said.

Bess nodded. She'd already thought through all of that. "As he should. I'm using our joint money to start this, and he hasn't complained once."

"But you're doing all of the work," Deb said, raising her hands in the air palms up.

"And he's supporting me. The same way I did for him in his career. This is my decision, Deb. And I may regret it one day, but I need to take this whole thing at my pace. I'm not going to hurry it along before I'm ready to because of the truck," Bess said as Gen and Olivia looked on.

Gen opened her mouth as if she wanted to say something but shut it when Bess shot her a look that begged her to stay out of it. Deb was full of anger, and Bess understood that. She was taking some of her anger about Rich out on Jon, which wasn't surprising. It wasn't even necessarily wrong. But Bess had it under control.

"I think you *will* regret it," Deb said.

"And I think I won't. So let's agree to disagree and move our conversation right along." Deb was still frowning. But she was no longer arguing, so Bess took that as consent.

"Did you know that Olivia and I got a new neighbor?" Bess asked.

Deb stopped frowning as hard as Gen added, "Yes, we heard. Dean Haskell. Whitney Barker sure is thrilled by it."

Deb's eyes softened with the change of subject. Now that they were no longer arguing, Bess saw the hurt that replaced the anger. She knew her friend was trying to protect her, and she loved her for it. Bess knew that even Gen wouldn't hold a grudge against Deb for her passionate railing against Jon. It was easy to see that Deb had first been hurt by Jon for Bess' sake and then even more cruelly by her own husband's betrayal. Even though Gen and Deb could fight with the best of them, at the end of the day, they loved one another.

"Of course Whitney is," Deb said with an eye roll that eased all of the tension in the room.

"Dean is a handsome man," Bess said, and she swore she saw a little tinge of pink brighten Olivia's cheeks.

"We all know Whitney doesn't have a set of brakes when a

handsome man is in her view," Gen said lightly, and the women laughed.

With the appearance of Deb's laugh and subsequent smile, Bess knew everything was okay. Bess shot a big one back at her friend to tell her all was well between the two of them. Deb gave Bess a slight nod—best friends didn't always need words—before turning back to the conversation at hand.

"Dean Haskell," Deb mused. "I guess he's one more man who isn't in the terrible camp. At least his six pack isn't. Too bad I'm not ten years younger."

"More like fifteen," Gen teased, and the women laughed again, filling Bess up with joy. Man, there were some bumps in their road. But she had a feeling they were all going to be okay.

THIRTEEN

OLIVIA PATTED HER STOMACH, still feeling full from the meal she'd eaten at Bess' home hours earlier. She'd somehow managed to get down a small salad at dinner. But she hadn't eaten seconds of any meal since before marrying Bart in an attempt to watch her figure. It felt good to be so full. She didn't want to do it all the time, but today it was exactly what she'd needed.

Rachel and Pearl had come home from school full of lots to say, and Olivia hadn't gotten a minute to herself until now—after school days had been thoroughly discussed, homework done and her girls happily in bed for the night.

Now that she was on her own, the conversation from the delicious lunch came back to her mind. She remembered Deb's strong opinion in opposition to all men and in support of a messy divorce, if need be. And then there was Bess' more peaceful approach to it all. Bess was even willing to share her hard work with a man who she thought would probably become her ex.

What did Olivia think about that?

She knew she didn't want to share anything with Bart. With a flip of her new, sassy, red hair, she felt empowered—not just from her hair but also from the words Gen had spoken. Olivia had been working hard at finding her worth. It was still definitely a work in progress, but she did know that she was worth more than giving Bart any more of herself. She'd done enough of that for years. Taking a step back helped her to see how much he'd crushed her in order to mold her into the woman he'd wanted, and she'd let him do that.

But no more. She wished it was as easy as wishing things would get better, but it wasn't. She still had moments where she wondered what Bart would think of a decision or where she let the callous words he'd often spoken bring her down, but she was trying. And trying meant she couldn't be like Bess. She could understand that it could be right for Bess and her life—Jon was a saint compared to Bart—but Olivia needed to stand up for herself and assert her rights more than Bess seemed to want to.

But did she want to be like Deb? That didn't seem for her either. Deb's headstrong manner in which she was taking on her divorce made it seem like she didn't even mind if there were casualties in the war she was waging against her ex. Olivia didn't want war. She just wanted what she deserved. She wanted her daughters to feel safe. And Olivia wanted her life back.

Maybe she was somewhere in the middle?

Olivia paused in her walk as she turned to the moonlit ocean and watched the dark waves lap up against the sand on the shoreline. She loved how different each of Whisling Island's beaches were. Some, like the cove she stood in, were covered in fine sand, the color appearing almost white in some lights. They allowed Olivia to imagine she was on some tropical island instead of Whisling. Not that there was anything wrong with Whisling. But she imagined on a tropical island she wouldn't need to have a sweater and jeans on as she walked the beach at night in mid-May. The beach by Bart's home had a mixture of rocks and sand, the sand rougher than the fine sand in the cove and also darker in color. The gray and sometimes even almost black sand felt like it was giving her feet a good scrubbing anytime she walked on that beach. And then there was the long stretch of beach by Elliot drive, the main area where tourists flocked because it was the type of beach Washington state was known for. Filled with rocks of every kind from white pebbles to huge gray boulders, her girls loved to spend their Saturdays searching through the rocks to find beautiful treasures. It did make for walking on the beach barefoot a little uncomfortable, but since Olivia had grown up going to rocky beaches, her feet had toughened up over the years. It was amazing how people adapted to their circumstances when they needed to.

"Wha—" Olivia jumped as she heard commotion beside her and turned to look at who or what had snuck up on her.

"I'm so sorry," Dean said as he laid a gentle hand on her shoulder. "I didn't mean to startle you. I was calling your name as I walked over, and I assumed you'd heard me."

"Nope," Olivia said, trying to smile as she calmed her rapidly beating heart. Their little cove was pretty private and never had any tourists, thanks to the secluded nature of it. But that didn't mean it was immune to bad things, and for a minute there, Olivia was certain a bad thing had just snuck up on her.

"Next time I'll be sure to keep calling your name, even when I think you've noticed me," Dean said.

Olivia nodded. That sounded like a good idea.

"If you want me to go ..." Dean began.

Olivia shook her head. This was his beach as much as hers. Maybe it was his even more than hers now since he'd bought a home here and she was still just living off her parents.

Living off her parents. Now that didn't have the best ring to it. She'd been in a trauma-induced fog for so long that she'd forgotten that it wasn't up to her parents to take care of her just because Bart wasn't. But with her new job, maybe she could finally get a leg up and hopefully stop free-loading sooner rather than later. Her parents both insisted they were in no hurry to get rid of her, but Olivia figured a plan of someday moving out would be for the best.

"It's your beach now, too." Olivia said the words she'd been thinking.

Dean smiled. "I've waited a long time for this place to be mine," he said.

Olivia turned to look at him. "Why the cove?" she asked. Dean had said he'd always admired Letman's Cove when they were at the park, but there were so many beaches on the island. Most of the island's residents dreamed of the wide rocky beaches that the tourists also loved to frequent.

"I'm not exactly sure. I remember coming out here when I came over to your house sometime during that summer before our junior year."

"Oh, I remember that night," Olivia said with a smile as she thought back to the night she'd had a bunch of friends over to watch a movie and play games in her family's living room. She hadn't realized Dean had escaped to the beach, but Olivia had been pretty preoccupied with Bart that night. It wasn't long after that party that he finally asked her to be his girlfriend.

"The whole place was so peaceful, even with all of us yelling right up there." Dean pointed to her parents' living room behind the hedges that separated the home from the sandy beach. "I told myself that someday I'd have a piece of that peace. It became an immediate dream."

"And you achieved it. Not many can say that while still the

young age of thirty-eight," Olivia said as she nudged Dean's shoulder with her own.

Dean chuckled. "I don't know that I'd attach the word *young* to our age anymore. I played basketball with a bunch of guys two days ago, and I'm still hurting."

It was Olivia's turn to giggle. Then she shook her head. "The aches and pains definitely aren't fun."

"Didn't you think we had a few more years before those set in?" Dean asked.

Olivia nodded. She'd assumed a lot of things about her life in her thirties that hadn't come to pass. "So are you just out here to reminisce about old times?" Olivia asked.

Dean watched her with an unreadable look on his face before nodding and saying, "I guess something like that."

Olivia looked ahead at the water splashing against the shore. The night Dean was remembering was the night of her first kiss with Bart. Her first kiss ever. For just a split second she allowed herself to wonder how her life would have gone if she'd come out here with Dean instead of staying in her kitchen with Bart. Olivia remembered the way Bart had taken her away from the rest of the group and told her he needed to talk to her about something important. But when they'd gotten to the kitchen, no words were exchanged. Just kisses. And Olivia was sure she was in love. But what if she'd escaped to the beach with her friend instead? Would she have never married Bart?

"I wonder what would've happened if I'd come out here that night instead ..." Olivia started, unsure of where her bravery had come from. That kind of statement and insight into her mind wasn't something that Olivia Birmingham usually gave. But she guessed now that she was Olivia Penn again, she'd have to reevaluate what she wanted to do and say as a whole new woman.

"That was the night that Bart first kissed you, right?" Dean asked.

Olivia wasn't sure why her cheeks burned in embarrassment.

"Sorry, I didn't mean to embarrass you. Bart and I were close back then. He was pretty thrilled after that kiss, and it didn't take long for him to share the news."

Olivia thought about that first kiss, how she'd also excitedly shared the news with her friends. Then her mind continued on to reminisce about her time with Bart in the years following. And even though she'd done so much of it wrong, she could never regret it. She had Rachel and Pearl, thanks wholly to her time with Bart.

"Oh no. That makes sense. It's just ... sometimes I forget how close you were with Bart. How close we all were," Olivia said softly.

She had been surprised when Bart had listed his groomsmen weeks into their wedding planning and Dean's name wasn't on the list. Granted, Dean had gone to a university a state away from where Bart and Olivia had gone to school, but they'd been so close in high school. When Bart and Dean didn't keep up their friendship, it almost seemed as if it wasn't an option for Olivia either. Bart and Dean had been the best friends. She'd just been a lucky side member of their group.

"Yeah. Sometimes it seems like a hundred years ago...." Dean said.

"And other times it seems like yesterday," Olivia finished.

Dean nodded. "So what were you out here thinking about?" Dean asked.

Olivia shrugged. It was crazy how easy it was to talk to Dean. But at the same time, she wondered if she'd already said too much about what she was going through. The last time she'd spoken with Dean at the park, she'd said more to Dean, now a near stranger, then she'd felt she could reveal to her own mother. But maybe that's what made talking to him so easy: the fact that he was now so distant from her life. Besides, the guy she'd known would've never judged her, and it seemed like this Dean had kept that quality about him. Dean made her feel safe. And that was something she'd been missing in spades.

"No way. I told you; now you have to tell me," Dean said as he nudged Olivia's shoulder.

Olivia laughed. "I know you were thinking about high school. But I didn't realize that meant you'd revert to acting like you're still in high school," Olivia teased before going right back to laughing.

Dean joined her laughter as he took a seat on the sand where they'd both been standing. Olivia watched as he dropped to the ground, grinning up at her in return.

"Sorry, but I wasn't joking. My muscles ache, and they're screaming at me to rest them," Dean said from his spot on the ground.

Olivia considered what to do for a split second before joining Dean on the sand so that they sat shoulder to shoulder. She wasn't ready to leave the beach yet, and talking to Dean was nice.

"Do you remember how often you and Bart would play basketball during that summer before our junior year? It was like seven hours straight," Olivia said.

"And then we'd spend the evening on the beach with the stupidest of us ending up in the water," Dean said.

"It was freezing!" Olivia exclaimed. "As I recall, you were in the ocean first, each and every time."

"Like I said, the stupidest of us," Dean said as he nudged Olivia's shoulder. "You didn't ever join us."

Olivia nodded. "Dang right I didn't. Like *I* said, it was freezing."

Dean laughed again, but Olivia fell silent. She'd forgotten about those nights, the bonfires that she'd stay at until her curfew. Those evenings had been before she'd started dating Bart, and it almost seemed like her life was divided into two parts: pre- and post-Bart. She'd pushed so much of the pre-Bart part out of her mind, probably in an effort to forget how different she'd been before Bart had decided what and who he wanted Olivia to be.

"I was thinking about the kind of woman I want to be during my divorce, and then who I want to continue to be after," Olivia said, answering the question Dean had asked awhile before. This time she spoke with much more forethought before revealing such an inner thought out loud to Dean. But even though it was scary to do so, it felt right. And she needed to talk to someone. Dean was here and he seemed willing to listen, so he was the lucky recipient of her innermost drama.

"That's pretty intense," Dean said, turning to look at Olivia. "So have you decided?"

Olivia nodded as she turned to look at the ocean. "I think so? It's just ... I never planned for this, you know? Even though Bart's been cheating on me since the beginning, and I should have been strong enough to leave then—"

"Wait, what?" Dean exclaimed so suddenly that Olivia had to look at him.

"I didn't plan on getting divorced—"

"No, the other part," Dean said.

"Bart was cheating on me? I thought everyone knew that. Especially after the reunion," Olivia said.

"I mean, I heard what happened that night. But ... it's been since the beginning?" Dean asked, his voice cracking.

Olivia nodded, amazed at how unemotional she was feeling at having to reveal this to Dean. She hoped this meant she'd finally come to terms with the years of abuse. Because that was what Bart had done to her. He'd pushed her away, abused her trust, and piled on verbal insults that would've made big, bad bikers blush.

"Meg. On the night before our wedding," Olivia said.

Dean stared at Olivia. He knew her bridesmaid who Bart had slept with, and his eyes were wide as if he couldn't quite believe what she was saying. He was taking quite a bit of time to digest it. Finally, he looked back at the water, shaking his head hard.

"He promised," Dean said, turning back to Olivia.

Olivia was surprised to see the emotion in Dean's eyes. "Who?" she asked.

"Bart. But the whole time? You deserve so much better, Liv," Dean said softly.

Olivia nodded, finally able to agree with Dean. She did. "What did Bart promise?" she asked.

Dean turned to the ocean, letting things fall silent between them for a minute before saying, "The same day as your first kiss. The afternoon before the party at your house."

Olivia nodded, hoping Dean would go on.

"We both liked you a lot," Dean said.

It was Olivia's turn to stare at the ocean. Dean had liked her? Her heart began to race with excitement until she reminded herself that just because Dean had liked her once upon a time, it didn't mean anything now. They were years and many experiences from the people they'd been then. And she had a feeling this story was about so much more than what Dean had once felt for her, so she focused on that instead of a childhood crush. Besides, it wasn't like Olivia was in a place where she could even think about dating again. But it did help her crushed ego a bit to know that Dean had thought of her in that way, even if it was a long time ago. Olivia played with a pebble under her hand as Dean kept going.

"It was our deal that neither of us would act on our feelings. The whole "friends before girls" kind of a thing. We both said we were happy having you as a friend, and we didn't want to ruin that." Dean spoke quietly, but fortunately the wind was calm so it was easy to hear even the softest of his words.

"I had no idea," Olivia said.

Dean nodded. "I assumed as much. Even though the entire male student body at Whisling High was in love with you."

"They were not," Olivia said as she swatted Dean's arm. Now he was just teasing her.

"They were. And Bart and I were no exception. We played ball that afternoon."

Of course they had. They were forever playing basketball. And Olivia had hated it because it was the one activity the guys always did without her.

"Bart told me his feelings for you had gotten stronger. I told him I felt the same. But he said he couldn't keep our pact anymore. He was in love with you."

Olivia felt her eyes go wide. Bart hadn't told her he loved her until graduation, nearly two years after that. If he had already loved her then, why had he waited so long to tell her? Or had he lied to Dean?

"I knew what I felt wasn't love. I didn't understand how he could feel love. But I didn't doubt him. He was my best friend. And if he was in love with you, I had to step back. So I did. But only after getting a promise from him that he'd be everything you needed and wanted."

"So you knew he was going to kiss me before the party?" Olivia asked.

"That's why I came to the beach. I couldn't stay in the same room where I knew I was losing my dream girl," Dean said.

Olivia felt a stab of sorrow in her heart. What would her life have been like if Bart hadn't broken that pact with Dean?

But then again, this was Bart. He would have found a way to what he wanted, no matter who or what was in the way. And back then he'd wanted Olivia. Hearing what Dean had said about the guys in high school, now it all made sense. Bart had always loved having what everyone else wanted. Back then it had been Olivia. He didn't want her because of who she was; he wanted her because she was wanted by the other guys. The thought made Olivia's stomach turn. Was that what her life with Bart for twenty years had been based on? The need to one up the other guys?

Olivia felt her breathing get shallow and her heart rate sped up drastically. As her body began to lose control she tried to concentrate on her life now, not go back to that place where Bart had controlled her and her emotions. What their relationship had been based on didn't matter anymore. He was gone, and she was out. She was safe.

Her breathing normalized, and she looked down to realize that Dean had taken both of her hands in his. He'd been her anchor during her panic attack.

"Thank you," she said as she pulled away her hands, feeling embarrassed that Dean had seen that. No one had witnessed her lose it; not her mom, not her girls, and definitely not Bart.

"Are you okay?" Dean asked, concern lining his face.

Olivia nodded. She shockingly was. Maybe it was from years of finding out nothing with Bart was as it seemed. This last revelation was startling, but no more than the other dozen or more she'd received in her marriage. Bart had proven early on how selfish he was. This was just another piece of evidence. But she would like to move the conversation right along.

"It's crazy how we can share day in and day out with a person and still find out these kinds of things, years down the line," Dean said.

Olivia nodded. It was crazy. But man, she was so done with this brand of crazy.

"My ex told me she didn't want to have kids." Dean picked up a rock and threw it toward the ocean.

"And you want them?" Olivia asked.

Dean nodded. "We were both professionals. Married to our jobs first. But that was only supposed to be the case until last year, when we'd been married for five years. Then we were supposed to try for kids. Yes, we planned this all out before we got married. How's that for romance?"

Olivia chuckled. Not because it was funny but because her laughter seemed to be what Dean needed to ease the tension his story brought to his shoulders. He gave her a hard smile before continuing.

"So we got to last year, and she told me she'd never planned on having kids. She was nearing thirty-five and felt too old to start a family. She figured I would come to feel the same way."

"But you didn't."

"I felt like everything we had was based on a lie. She didn't understand why we couldn't continue on in our lives the way they were. I think, in her own way, she loved me. But when I came home for the reunion, I remembered the guy I'd been back here. Dean from high school would have hated Dean in his thirties. He would have looked at my life and thought it was a waste. Sure, my career was thriving. But besides that, I had a woman who maybe loved me in her own way and no chance at a family. I went to the gym five days a week, but I didn't even play basketball anymore."

Olivia smiled.

"So I left it all. I left her. She didn't cry, and I knew I'd made the right decision. We had both settled, and we would only continue to hurt one another. I heard about the house on this street, and I jumped at the chance."

"Are you happy now?" Olivia asked as she watched a set of three waves come into shore.

"I think I'm getting there. What about you?"

Olivia nodded slowly. "I'm a lot closer than I was before."

Dean turned to face her. "Here's to new beginnings then."

"And finally finding that happiness."

FOURTEEN

"I HATE YOU!" Bailee screamed as she slammed the door shut behind her and sped off to school.

Deb wished she could say this was an abnormal occurrence, but she and her daughter had lived this scene a number of times since Rich had left her. Deb knew she was wound tight, and Bailee was the one hurting the most because of it. But she had no idea what to do.

This time the "I hate you" had stemmed from the fact that Deb wouldn't let Bailee go on a coed camping trip with her new boyfriend. And because of the reason, for once Deb wore the *I hate you* badge with honor. She was okay with Bailee hating her because she was looking out for the best interests of her young and impressionable daughter. It was some of the past "I hate you"s that had stung more.

The one that came right after a particularly bad call with Rich where Deb had drunk more than the couple glasses of wine she was used to and Bailee had tried to stick up for her dad. Deb had let loose, telling Bailee just what her precious dad had been doing in the time since he'd moved to London. Deb had watched her little girl crumble, and drunk Deb had told her it was for her daughter's own good. Sober Deb regretted that night with a passion, and since then, she'd stopped drinking. Alcohol and anger didn't mix well, and there weren't many days when Deb wasn't angry.

Deb walked into her studio and gazed at the two paintings she'd been working on. Both were full of reds, oranges, and blacks, her sweet sunset painting all but forgotten. Even her art felt angry.

Deb felt the rush of adrenaline and the burst in her chest that always occurred after she found yet another thing Rich had affected in her life. She was about to relish in the emotion that had kept her sane for these past few weeks. But then she paused, thoughts of her sweet daughter and her ruined art leading the charge that there may be another way for her to deal with this chaos.

After talking with the women at Bess' house the day before, Deb had driven home wondering if there was a way to do this without all of the anger. It hadn't even occurred to her before because anger was better than pain. At least while she was this mad, there was no room for anything else.

However, the anger also left little room to love her daughter, to be there for her friends, and even her work was suffering. Who was she helping by avoiding her pain? Definitely not any of the three aforementioned. And definitely not herself.

This had to stop. She had to let the anger go. But that was much easier said than done. Especially with Rich still behaving like such a prick.

But did she have to behave this way just because Rich was? Was she reverting back to playground rules? He kicked Deb so Deb had to kick him? She knew she kind of was. She was reacting instead of acting, something she'd always warned her children not to do.

What was her goal? To get Rich out of her life ... as quickly as possible. But their fighting was just prolonging things. She'd done plenty of immature things just to stick it to Rich, but since she'd finally figured out a way to get the hundred thousand Rich was asking for, wasn't it time to just give in and move on? Even though it wasn't what she wanted to do, maybe she should just do it? To be done with this and fast track this thing all the way to the courthouse? Because maybe if she wasn't working so hard at being angry with Rich, she could find the time and energy to love and raise her daughter for the few months she had left. Shame and regret filled Deb as she realized that graduation was just a few weeks away and that this might be the last summer she'd have Bailee on Whisling. If Bailee left for college feeling this animosity toward her mother, would Deb lose her daughter?

The thought left her feeling panicked, and Deb didn't care what it cost. Everything had to change ... now.

"Hey, Doug," Deb said when her attorney answered her call.

"Deb," Doug said cautiously, and Deb couldn't blame him. She'd reamed him out the last few times she'd spoken to him.

"He can have it," Deb said. This divorce had become like a noose around her neck, getting tighter with every tug from Rich and also from herself. Moving on meant getting out of the noose. Deb needed out.

"Rich?" Doug clarified.

Deb answered in the affirmative. "I'll take the money out of my equity. I just want out," she said.

Doug murmured something that sounded like *finally*.

"Can I get out of this marriage? Now?" Deb asked, filled with an emotion she hadn't felt for all too long: hope.

"This was Rich's last big hang up, so I think we should be good. I'll be sure to let them know they are lucky to be getting this deal, and this is the best it's going to get. Once they've agreed, I'll pull some strings to get it fast tracked."

"When will it be final?" Deb asked. She felt the urgent need to move on today, but she doubted it would happen that fast.

"As long as Rich and his attorney agree to things, I can email the papers over to you later today. That won't be the last of it, but it will be close." Doug said the exact words Deb had only hoped to hear. It wouldn't be finalized, but she'd start the final steps that very day. That felt like enough for Deb. Could Doug feel her need to move on immediately? She knew that probably wasn't the case, but he still deserved every penny of his fee.

"Thank you, Doug," Deb said before hanging up the phone and falling into the one chair she kept in her art studio.

She'd allowed her anger at Rich to rule her for so long that everything in her life had been rimmed with a red haze. She took in a deep breath and let it out. She was finally ready to let that go.

She knew the change wouldn't be immediate, but wanting to have her life be a little less rage-filled was a step in the right direction. Deb needed to take the next steps now, which for her would be a nice, long run. Then she needed to be ready for Bailee when she got home from school. The poor girl needed to know her mother, the one who loved her and put her above all else, was back for good.

"WHY?" Bailee eyed Deb cautiously after Deb asked her if she wanted to go out for a pizza.

"Because we haven't spent much time together in the last few months," Deb said.

"That isn't my fault," Bailee countered with a sassy tilt of her head. Deb deserved that.

"I know. I'm sorry, Bails. I've been a terrible mom these past couple of months, and I know I can't make that up to you. But I want to try hard to be better ... starting right now."

Bailee's eyes narrowed. "Why now?"

It only stung for a few seconds that Bailee hadn't even tried to pretend that Deb had been anything but terrible. Bailee was usually the first to give Deb the benefit of the doubt. The fact that she so readily agreed with Deb just showed how far gone Deb had been. But Deb couldn't let guilt over her past actions lead her now; that wouldn't help Bailee. She would start being a better mom, asap.

"Because it took your idiot mother this long to see what this was doing to you. What I was doing to you." Deb was just grateful her son was no longer living at home, and she hoped she wasn't too late to fix things with Bailee.

"Got sick of sticking it to Dad?" Bailee asked with a hand on her hip.

"Got sick of hurting you," Deb said, and she noticed the hard purse of Bailee's mouth soften.

"Fine. But we're getting pepperoni," Bailee said, knowing it was her mother's least favorite topping.

"Got it," Deb said, struggling to hide her smile. She knew Bailee would only see that as a sign of victory and might back out if she thought she was losing to her mom. But Deb hoped from now on no one would be losing in their household. She really hoped they could all be winners.

FIFTEEN

GEN PATTED her stomach the way she'd seen expectant mothers do for years. But this time Gen had a sliver of a reason to do so. She was late for her period, and like too many months in her past, she wondered if this was it. She and Levi had tried invitro and practically every other infertility treatment there was. She began to care less for the risks she was taking with her own life if only she could fill her womb with a babe. But it hadn't happened. Month after month, year after year. And the likelihood that today was her day was slim. But what if? Miracles happened, right?

"Hey, Gen," Kate, her receptionist, said as she poked her head into Gen's office.

Gen let her hand drop from her stomach.

"Levi's here to see you." Kate grinned, and Gen returned her smile.

Gen swore half of her salon was in love with her husband, but she didn't mind because Levi only had eyes for her. It hadn't always been that way, but through years of therapy she could honestly say she completely and fully trusted her husband to stay true to her and only her.

The thought of therapy almost always reminded Gen why they had been there. She recalled the days, weeks, and months of crying after finding out that Levi had slept with another woman. Granted, looking back now, she knew it wasn't solely his fault. Gen had just miscarried her second IVF attempt and was broken. Physically, emotionally, she was empty in every way. She had nothing left for herself much less the man she loved. So she told Levi it was over. She told him she couldn't be married to him anymore and asked for a divorce. Keeping Levi from having a child was one of the worst parts of all of this. She thought, maybe, without her, he could have all that he dreamed of. He deserved more than her.

Even after her screaming and kicking him out, Levi attempted to come home every night for two weeks. But every night she sent him away in the same dramatic manner, telling him to never return. So one night he didn't. He ended up at a bar and drank way too much. He left the bar with a woman and regretted that action every day since.

Gen believed his regret. She also believed he would never do it again, and she knew in her heart he'd only acted out of grief. He had also lost the chance at a child, but instead of finding solace in his wife, she'd pushed him away. It didn't excuse his action, and it took Gen a long time to forgive him and rebuild that trust, but now she was so glad that she had. She and Levi were stronger than ever. There wasn't much they couldn't withstand as a team.

Levi stepped through her office door, and Gen felt butterflies flit in her stomach. Levi Redding was as handsome as men came. His sandy blonde hair was a bit longer than he liked to keep it, the stray hairs constantly falling into his light green eyes. But he knew his wife appreciated the look, so he didn't cut his hair quite as often as he used to. He was a good nearly foot taller than her five two, and she felt he was the perfect height, especially when they kissed. His broad shoulders were what had women falling for him ever since high school, and they'd only broadened further thanks to his years in construction. She grinned at her husband. Fifteen years of marriage and she still anticipated his touch.

But when Gen focused in on Levi's face, she noticed his severe frown. Levi was the happiest man she knew. He was always smiling. Why wasn't he smiling?

He shut the door behind him and his frown continued as he took the seat across from where Gen sat at her desk, not coming around to kiss her the way he normally would.

What was going on?

After he sat, she looked at him, trying to figure out what emotions his face expressed. She realized he wouldn't look at her. His eyes scanned her tiny office about a hundred times, but he never let them rest on Gen.

"Levi?" Gen finally voiced the concern she was feeling. Whatever was coming wasn't good, but she had to know what was going on.

She watched as her husband's Adam's apple bobbed, a sure sign that he was nervous. Then he finally met her eyes.

"I don't know how to say this, Gen," Levi said, and then he dropped his eyes again, allowing Gen to figure out exactly what Levi was feeling. Shame.

What had he done?

Gen realized she had about two seconds before Levi told her the truth, and she had a huge decision to make. She had no idea what was going to come out of his mouth. But she could do one of two things after hearing his shameful revelation. She could push him away. The way she had years before. Or she could hear him out and try to work things out.

Gen decided, even before Levi uttered another word, she was going to do the latter. She loved the man sitting at her desk, and she would do anything for him. Including claw their way to a good place in their marriage again. That revelation made her feel more at ease as she waited for his next words.

"She had a baby," Levi said, and now Gen was just lost. Who had a baby? And why did Levi feel shame about it? Realization hit her like a Mack truck.

"*You* have a baby," Gen said softly, her chest tightening in a way that made it hard for her to breathe.

"I don't know that she's mine."

"It's a girl?" Gen asked, looking down at her own belly that had so far produced nothing of worth. Gen fought back a sob. She had to keep the emotion at bay for now. She needed answers before she fell apart. Gen worked to take an emotional step away from the situation. If she could pretend that this was happening to someone else, maybe she could make it through this conversation without completely breaking down.

"Gen, I can get a paternity test. The likelihood that this child is mine ..."

Gen raised her hand, causing Levi to stop speaking. She felt like she was missing a piece to the puzzle, and she needed a specific question answered immediately. She had a feeling this question would give her the piece she needed. "Why now, Levi? This happened three years ago. She's had over two years to say something."

"She's sick," Levi said.

Gen felt her heart drop. She'd been expecting anything but that. Sick? What did that mean? "The baby?" Gen asked, suddenly deeply afraid for the welfare of this baby.

Levi shook his head. "Mal," he said, voicing the name the two of them had decided neither of them would ever utter again.

Against the suggestion of their therapist, Levi and Gen had decided together that the night with Mal held too many painful memories for them to ever work through. So they put it behind them, without really talking about it. There had seemed to be no need since Gen had truly forgiven Levi, and Levi knew he'd never make the same mistake again. They hadn't needed to talk it out. But it looked like that night wouldn't go unforgotten.

Gen shook her head free of the memories of the past. There was plenty enough in the present to deal with.

"How sick?" Gen asked.

"Stage four lymphoma," Levi whispered. "It's terminal."

Gen felt terror at those words and suddenly realized this emotion she was feeling wasn't for herself; it was for a baby girl who had a sick mother. Did this mean Gen cared about this child she'd never met? One that might be a part of her husband but not a part of her?

"So why come to you now if she didn't want you to know about the baby earlier?" Gen asked as she threaded a hand through her hair, trying to grasp onto something that was normal even while it felt like her world was spinning out of control.

"She knew about you, Gen. I guess I wouldn't stop talking about you that night, and she's felt guilty ever since. But now that her time is so short ... she's trying to right her wrongs. She wants Maddie to know her dad," Levi said, looking everywhere in the room but at Gen.

Levi was a father. The words settled into Gen's soul as her heart and gut clenched, a pain like no other filling her.

"She might not be mine, Gen." Levi's expression immediately went from ashamed to worried. "I can get a paternity test—"

"Really, Levi? Because from where I sit, an alternative seems impossible. If Mal thought there was any chance the father wasn't you, wouldn't she have gone to those men first? She stayed away for three years because she didn't want to disturb our lives due to the guilt she's felt. Maddie is yours, Levi." Gen said the words forcefully, knowing she had to get this thought through her husband's head. He was all this baby was going to have left.

It all became too much as Gen felt a sob tear through her and escape her lips.

"Gen. I'm so sorry, Gen. If I could go back and change things ..." Levi stood and traversed the short distance between them before pulling Gen into his arms.

Gen cried against the strong shoulder that typically kept all of the bad in the world at bay. But now it felt like they were right back to where they'd been three years before, and Gen couldn't go back there.

"I don't have to do this. Nothing has to change," Levi said.

Gen pushed against his shoulders so that she put some space between them. "*Everything* has changed, Levi. This is your daughter. There is no choice in the matter," she said, now feeling anger on top of her sorrow. She'd take anger any day.

"We always have choices, Gen. And I choose you. Today and every day," Levi said softly.

Gen nodded as more tears rolled down her cheeks; her anger had been short-lived.

"But she's your daughter, Levi. She's a baby that has no one," Gen said.

Levi shook his head. "Mal's parents are happy to take the baby in. It's what they want," he said.

Now Gen understood what Levi was saying about options. But could Levi live with himself, knowing he had a child out in the world who he would never know? Could Gen live with that?

"What does Mal want?" Gen asked because she knew she didn't have to ask what Levi wanted. He wanted anything Gen wanted. She truly believed that.

"She loves her parents and had a spectacular childhood but thinks Maddie deserves parents of her own." Levi's words were staccato, as if he didn't want them to come out. But because Gen asked, he had to give them.

Gen held her stomach as she walked to the one window in the room, pushing the yellow curtains aside to look at the view of the quaint main drive of the island. She could have chosen to have her salon on the other side of the road and have an ocean view, but Gen liked that she got nearly two times the space right where she was for the same price.

"You have to take her in, Levi," Gen said.

But Levi shook his head. "Not without you, Gen. I need you."

"How can you say that? She needs you," Gen said.

Levi shook his head again. "Not like you need me," Levi said softly. "I have to put you first."

Gen knew Levi was trying to do what was right, but the situation was just horrible enough that no solution felt right.

Gen already knew what she needed to do. Hadn't Gen just told herself she would work things out with Levi no matter what came out of his mouth? She would've never dreamed this would be his revelation, but she knew what she wanted, what she needed. She needed Levi. Even with a baby that wasn't hers. Even if they may never have a baby of their own. Gen squared her shoulders resolutely.

"Tell Mal we want Maddie." Gen said each word slowly, her throat constricting around them. But she had to say them.

"Gen ..."

"We, Levi. I mean it. I don't like it, but I mean it," Gen said as Levi walked closer to Gen and then fell to his knees, taking Gen's hands in his.

"Gen, I wish—"

"Don't finish whatever you were going to say. Please," Gen whispered, and Levi nodded because they both knew wishes meant nothing.

Gen drew in a deep breath, knowing what had to come next. Levi wasn't going to like this part, but the logistics of how this would all go had come to Gen immediately. It was what Levi had always called her gift. Gen could navigate herself out of any situation, but today it didn't feel much like a gift and way more like a curse. Because her insight into logistics told Gen her future would be vastly different from the one she'd imagined with Levi. Forever.

"I'm going to stay with Bess for a while," Gen said, pulling her hands out of Levi's grasp.

"No," Levi said as he stood.

"I meant what I said. This is going to be 'we.' But Mal needs to be with her baby for her last days, and you need to get to know Maddie immediately. I can't be in the house while that's happening."

"They don't have to stay at the house," Levi said.

"You would let that baby lose her mom and her home all in one day? Let Maddie get to know our house, and I will raise her with you. But this transition has to be without me," Gen said. Then she let her forehead fall to the glass of her window, her eyes focusing on the bustling tourists and locals just outside of her salon.

Other people. Gen just realized the population of the island was going to have some severe opinions about what was going on in Gen's home, now that they would all know her truth. She'd kept Levi's indiscretion a secret for years, but not anymore. However, what was done was done. She wouldn't let a sweet, innocent baby suffer so that she could save face. It was time to woman up and put the needs of someone else in front of hers, even if that meant ruining the image of their marriage.

"Gen, I'm sorry," Levi said.

Gen nodded against the glass. She knew. But right now, sorry did nothing.

"Are we going to be okay?" Levi asked.

Gen didn't know what to say. "I'll try to work through this. We'll try." That was all Gen could give him.

"That's more than I deserve," Levi said.

"No, it's not. I already forgave you for that night. That means I have to already forgive you for this. But I just ... it's a lot at once, you know? So let me have time to process while you transition. I'll come home again ..." Gen couldn't say, "After Mal leaves," because Mal leaving would be the end of the world for the baby Gen would have to find it in her heart to love.

She shook her head. There was too much to take in at once.

"Can I call you?" Levi asked.

Gen paused, thinking her words through carefully before saying, "Maybe text?"

Levi nodded fervently as he said, "Every day."

Gen suddenly felt the enormity of giving her husband away, even if it was temporary. Because when Gen moved back home, a part of him would be permanently given to Maddie. She knew Levi too well to not know this would be the case. But could Gen share him? She had to.

"I love you, Gen," Levi whispered as he came behind her and hugged her in a way that told Gen he was holding on, telling her he wasn't going to ever let her go.

"I can't say it now," Gen said. When she saw Levi's anguished expression in the reflection of the window she added, "But I'm not giving up. And now you have to go to your daughter."

Gen swallowed and then stepped out of Levi's arms, and immediately she felt lost. Even though this mess was thanks to Levi's actions, he was her anchor.

Levi headed for the door and then stopped just before opening it.

"I love you, Gen Redding," he said.

Gen nodded before he turned and left her office.

With Levi gone, Gen no longer had to be strong. She no longer had to come up with solutions. She fell to the ground and held her stomach as she cried. She cried for Levi and Maddie. She even cried for Mal. But most of all, she just cried for herself.

SIXTEEN

"SO ALL THAT'S left is to open the doors?" Bess asked Olivia as they sat at her kitchen table—the place that had become command central for their food truck operation in the past couple of weeks since Bess had hired Olivia.

"Well, you still have to stock the pantry and fridge, but the legal side of it is all done. We are approved as a business in the greater Seattle area and on Whisling Island," Olivia said with a grin.

Bess returned Olivia's smile with gusto. Ever since Gen had come to live with her the week before, Bess hadn't been smiling much. Between her sister's pain and the stress of the truck, Bess hadn't had much reason to smile. But today was different.

They were moving forward with their business. It was a good thing, too, since Olivia had announced to social media and the couple of small, local news outlets that cared that they would be having their grand opening in just over a week, the night before the high school's graduation. Bess figured it would be the perfect time to get lots of business between families being in town for the big event along with peak tourist season following right behind.

"We did it," Bess said as she leaned back in her seat, suddenly feeling exhausted. Whether from what she'd done or what was coming, she didn't know.

"You did," Olivia said.

"Oh no. You'd better not sell yourself short, Olivia. I couldn't have done any of this without you," Bess said passionately.

Olivia gave a small nod. "Thank you for this opportunity," she said, causing Bess to remember the words she'd spoken soon after Bess had hired her. Olivia had been having a hard time finding purpose for a long time, but especially after she'd left Bart. The food truck and all of the work it needed had been her salvation, or so she'd said, and Bess was only too grateful to be a small part of Olivia's process. She knew Olivia's divorce was almost final.

"Thank you for saving me. This whole thing was a mess before you and your organizational skills," Bess said.

Olivia laughed because she knew that was the truth. Then she got up, gathering her things.

As Bess watched Olivia, her eyes fell to the picture just behind Olivia: Bess' wedding portrait. Speaking of moving on, she really needed to take that down. She also needed to talk to Doug again. She'd taken the first steps of separation but hadn't pushed anything else to go forward. She knew Jon wouldn't either. So if they were going to get divorced, it was up to Bess. And most days she was ninety percent sure this was what she needed. But that ten percent nagged her to just be happy with where she was. Jon was giving her space, and the food truck was taking all of her time. But all of those were just excuses. Bess needed to make a decision. Her marriage deserved that.

Bess looked away from the portrait as she heard the sound of slippers moving across her hardwood floor, and she looked at the hallway just in time to see Gen emerging.

"Olivia, Bess," Gen said as she made her way to the fridge,

her robe flapping at her sides revealing the t-shirt and pj pants she still wore. It was two pm, and Gen was still in her pajamas. But she was choosing to eat on her own, which Bess was going to take as a win. For the first two days Gen had been there, Bess had had to practically force feed her.

"Things looking good for the truck?" Gen asked as she closed the fridge and moved to a container of cannolis on the counter.

Okay, so maybe eating was a broad word for what Gen was doing. Maybe desserting was a better explanation.

"They are," Olivia said as she took a cannoli from the open container Gen held. "We're opening next week."

"Seriously? So soon?" Gen asked before taking a large bite.

"It's been on the calendar for a while, so I think we'll be ready," Bess said as she enjoyed the view of the women loving her food. There was no greater feeling than making something that others loved.

"Has it? I'm sorry, Bess. It must have slipped my mind. I swear the days feel like weeks, but now I wonder where the last week has gone," Gen said.

Bess completely understood the feeling.

"See you both tomorrow," Olivia said as she slipped out. The woman had a sixth sense for knowing when a conversation should be private and, per usual, was giving Bess and her sister the space they needed.

"You've been a little preoccupied. Speaking of which, is the salon okay?" Bess asked.

Gen nodded. "Kate's incredible, and she rescheduled everything she could. Whatever she couldn't, my stylists covered, even coming in on their days off. I didn't realize what a crack team I have. I guess some good has come out of my life imploding so publicly." Gen tried to smile, but it looked like a grimace.

"I'm glad. And are you okay?" Bess had to ask the question weighing on her mind.

"Okay is such a relative term. But I'm functioning. I'm alive and healthy. I haven't thrown up in a day," Gen said, and Bess nodded.

That had been a weird side effect to Gen's grief that neither of them had been expecting. Gen had thrown up once a day since showing up on Bess' doorstep, completely devastated. Bess was still having a hard time wrapping her mind around the events that had unfolded in Gen's life. Bess had had no idea Levi had stepped out on their marriage, but after Gen had explained things, she could see why Gen had kept the events away from the rest of the world. And they'd somehow worked through it all. Even Gen's infertility and the pain that had caused both of them. Only to be hit with this. But Bess couldn't help but think that any baby was a blessing, and she hoped this baby girl would somehow be one for both Levi and Gen.

"And I'm going to go back to work," Gen said, and Bess felt her eyes go wide. "Tomorrow. I have to. They need me, and I'm over wallowing."

Bess nodded. Grief had a unique way for each person. If Gen was working through hers in a way Bess didn't understand, there was nothing strange about that. Just like she was sure Gen didn't agree with the way Bess was handling her own, granted Bess wasn't sure Bess agreed with the way she was handling her grief.

"But for now, I'm going to go back to bed and enjoy the rest of these." Gen took the container of cannolis with her as she went back down the hall.

Bess heard the bedroom door close before her eyes went back to the wedding portrait and the emotions she'd felt on that incredible day. She remembered waiting outside the doors of the church, shifting from one foot to the other and practically gnawing off her lipstick because she was so nervous. But then the doors opened and she saw Jon. Handsome, reliable Jon. The man in that picture. And she felt complete calm. Because Jon was her security, her safety through the tempest.

But now? Bess felt tears roll down her cheeks and was suddenly fueled by a rage that kind of scared her. How could he do this? How could he break all that they had? And for what?

Bess grabbed her phone, ready to give Jon a piece of her mind, let him know just how severely his actions had wounded her. Then she thought better of it. She needed to chew Jon out in person.

THE FERRY RIDE had gone all too fast. Bess was now in an Uber on her way to Jon's new apartment. He'd given her the address in case of an emergency—probably not for the reason she was seeking him out, but tough luck for Jon.

Bess' rage continued as she rode. She was barely able to thank her Uber driver for the ride, and she slammed the door of the apartment building behind her as she walked up the three stories of steps, only adding more rage to her fire. Why couldn't Jon have chosen a building with an elevator? Now she was going to be out of breath as she screamed her frustrations at him.

Bess knocked firmly on the door and worried for a split second that Jon wouldn't be there, but the door opened and Jon's face appeared in front of her. He looked worn out, and under his black-rimmed glasses, his eyes looked red. But good, he deserved red eyes.

"How could you?" Bess said from the middle of the doorway.

"Bess?" Jon looked from Bess to the hallway behind her. "Do you want to come in?"

Bess realized her yelling session would probably best be

done in private, so she walked in the doorway enough to close the door behind her before starting again. "I loved you. I adored you. For thirty years!"

"I know," Jon said.

Bess shoved him and then felt her eyes go wide at the same time Jon's did. Bess didn't do physical violence, but she had to admit it kind of felt good.

"It's my turn to speak," Bess said forcefully, and Jon nodded. "I made your lunches, ironed your shirts, went to your stupid academia parties. I raised our children, I kept a clean home, I made your favorite dinners. I should have been enough," Bess said, suddenly leaning against the door behind her and feeling tears spring to her eyes. Where had her rage gone?

"You were," Jon began.

Bess raised a hand. "Not your turn."

Jon nodded again.

"We were supposed to have forever, Jon. You broke that. You broke us. And I don't think I can forgive you for that."

Jon nodded even as tears streamed down his face.

"I have to go forward with our divorce. I think a part of me was hoping our past would be enough for me to push through the hurt and pain. But I can't, Jon. I don't have another chance to give you." Bess could hardly see Jon, her tears coming so fast and strong. She was going to get a divorce. She was going to no longer be married to Jon. Her Jon would no longer be her Jon.

"I can't love you anymore," Bess said, and Jon fell against the counter behind him.

"Bess."

"I can't, Jon. I tried, and I can't." Bess shook her head once and then opened the door behind her.

And even as sorrow threatened to overwhelm her, a small part of Bess felt lighter. She had done the right thing. But that didn't make it hurt any less.

SEVENTEEN

GEN HAD SURVIVED LITERALLY the longest day of her life. She assumed the worst was behind her, but she should have known their patrons at the salon wouldn't let her off so easy. She'd been consoled when she didn't want to be and asked nearly a hundred times if she was going to leave Levi, along with other well-meaning but completely unwanted communications.

She sat down at her desk, knowing she needed to decompress before going back to Bess'. Her sister didn't deserve all of the crap she'd been dished recently, and Gen hated that she'd added to it. But she'd needed her big sister. However, today she was going to look out for Bess and make sure she was in a better frame of mind before she went back to Bess' home.

The last conversation had hit Gen the hardest. Eleanor Mason had met Mal ... and Maddie.

"She's the sweetest little girl, Gen," Eleanor had said. "And I know everyone here has made Mal the enemy ... and they should. I'm team Gen all the way. But seeing the woman. She's so frail, Gen. I can't help but feel sorry for her."

Gen had felt tears rise to her eyes. She might be nursing a heart that had once again been fissured, but Mal was looking death in the face. Even heartache couldn't keep Gen from knowing Mal had the far worse end of the stick. What would it be like to know you were going to leave the person you loved most? For life. Gen couldn't imagine that sort of pain. And the trust Mal must have in Levi. Levi must've shown Mal what a good-hearted man he was, even at his lowest moment.

Gen swallowed back the nausea that hit every time she thought about Levi with Mal. She'd thrown up again at work that morning. She was definitely over this stage of grief. She would be happy to never throw up again.

She stood, suddenly realizing what she needed to do for herself and for everyone else in this situation. She needed to meet Maddie. See Mal. Come face to face with the woman who Gen was sure had torn up their lives. But in hindsight, Gen knew they'd all played a role. Maybe some were bigger roles in their tragedy, but none were free of blame.

Except for Maddie.

Gen gathered her purse and keys before she could chicken out. Her car took the road home, and before she knew it, Gen was parked in the driveway of the home she'd shared with Levi for fifteen years.

He'd been true to his word and given Gen her space. His sweet texts hadn't stopped, even when Gen didn't return any of Levi's sentiments because, even with all that he had to say to Gen, she had nothing to return to him. At least not yet.

She turned off the engine and watched the home for signs of life. There was a big picture window to the left of the driveway, but in the twilight hours of the evening, Gen wasn't able to see anything inside since Levi hadn't turned on the lights yet.

But she knew they were all at home. A car she didn't recognize sat parked at the curb behind her, and Levi's work truck sat next to where she'd parked in the driveway. Gen usually took the garage, but for some reason, she didn't want to use the access that she had to the home. She felt like she'd be infringing on Mal's and Levi's rights if she just barged in. Which was crazy because it was her house. But it didn't feel right. Not much about this did.

However, coming to meet Maddie was something that felt right. The first thing that had felt right since the day Levi had come to her office. And that was how she found the strength to finally open her car door and walk up the blue, flower-lined path to her front door.

She raised her hand to the doorbell, but the door opened before she could press it.

Levi stood in front of her, the lines on his face looking a little deeper than the last time Gen had seen him. His eyes were red as if he wasn't sleeping well, but he was dressed and clean-shaven, telling Gen he was trying to put on a brave face. Probably for his daughter.

"Gen," Levi whispered, and Gen nodded. She was there. But now she had no idea what she was supposed to do.

Levi met her eyes, and he hesitated for a split second before pulling Gen into his arms and wrapping her in a hug she had sorely missed. Even with their ups and downs, even with every hardship she'd endured, she knew this was still where she belonged. Because as much as a part of her wanted to run away, escape the madness that was her life right now—it would've probably been easier—she couldn't. Her commitment to Levi went beyond these hardships. She was willing to work for the man she loved. She knew Levi would do anything for her as well. Because even though they both made mistakes, they both wanted the course that led back to the other. That was the only reason Gen had any hope they would work.

"I think I need to meet Maddie," Gen said bravely from within Levi's arms. Because in his arms, she felt like she could do anything.

Levi continued to hold her tight, and she had a feeling he wouldn't let go until she made him.

"Are you sure?" he asked. "You don't have to do this for me."

"I know. I have to do this for me." Gen felt her eyes fill with tears, but she drew in a deep breath, trying to push her emotions down. It wouldn't do to scare the baby.

"Do you think Mal will be okay with that?" Gen asked, even as her stomach twisted. A part of her would never like Mal, even though she knew she should be a bigger person and forgive the woman. She was dying, for goodness' sake. Gen had forgiven Mal to an extent, but she knew she'd always see Mal as the woman who had almost broken their marriage and broken her. Mal had known Levi was married, and she'd been sober when she took Levi home. That didn't excuse Levi, and Gen had been every bit as upset with Levi as she had been with Mal. But she'd had to forgive Levi to move on. Mal, not so much. Especially because she knew nothing about the woman other than that she'd slept with her husband. But now she guessed she was getting to know another side of the woman, even without meeting her. She seemed to be an excellent mom, putting the needs of her daughter before her own. And that was why Gen felt the need to get Mal's approval. Gen had to respect that Mal was and would always be Maddie's mom.

Gen looked up at Levi to see him nodding his head. "She wants you to help raise Maddie. I think that means you have to meet her."

"Mal wants that?" Gen asked.

"She knows we're a package deal, Gen. Asking me to be in Maddie's life meant asking you," Levi said.

"But she doesn't even know me."

"She apparently knows enough. I'm guessing it has something to do with the fact that you were able to forgive me and that you haven't gone on a vendetta to get back at Mal. Also, since she's been here, the entire island has been singing your praises," Levi said.

"They haven't been too hard on Mal, have they?" Gen asked.

"Not that she's mentioned," Levi said, and Gen nodded against his chest. She suddenly felt the weirdest urge to want to protect Mal. Which was insane. But Mal was trusting Gen with the greatest part of her, and that trust went a long way in helping Gen to see Mal as a fellow woman instead of "the other woman."

"Outside, Daddy?" an angel voice said from the foyer behind Levi, and Gen had to pull out of Levi's arms. This little girl was calling her husband daddy, and Gen immediately felt a love like no other overwhelm her as her eyes filled with tears again.

Levi turned around just in time to grab the toddling girl with the most gorgeous strawberry blonde hair before she ran out of the doorway.

"Gen, this is Maddie," Levi said, and Gen itched to carry this perfect little girl.

Maddie gave Gen a huge grin and then lunged out of her father's arms toward Gen.

"I think she wants to meet you," Levi said with a laugh as he let Maddie crawl out of his arms and into Gen's.

Gen embraced the adorable girl, and her heart felt near to bursting. She had heard moms talk about the first time they held their child and connecting with them at first sight. Gen had wondered if she would ever experience that. And now she was.

"Hey, Maddie. I'm Gen," Gen said.

Maddie stared up at Gen before taking her chubby hand and wrapping it in Gen's brown curls. "Den," Maddie said happily as she continued to play with Gen's hair.

"She hasn't quite gotten her g sounds down yet," Levi whispered.

"I picked up on that," Gen said, her smile only growing

larger. This little girl was perfect.

"Do you want to go on a walk? Get to know Maddie?" Levi offered.

Gen shook her head. She knew she had one more thing she had to do that evening, and she really wanted to get it over with before she chickened out.

Gen stepped into her home and took the short hall from the foyer that led to the living room and kitchen where she was sure Mal had to be waiting.

She gave Maddie to Levi before she rounded the bend that would take her into the living room. Then she took a deep breath before taking those last steps.

Mal sat on Gen's couch tentatively. Her butt was on the edge of the seat and her elbows rested against her knees. The position looked uncomfortable, and the fact that Mal had to be fatigued from the cancer that was taking over her body made Gen feel like she had to say something before even meeting the woman.

"Please take a better seat," Gen said, and Levi laughed, causing Gen to replay her words. They had been a bit strange.

"Um," Mal said, and Gen sat on the other end of the same couch, leaning back in her seat the way she hoped Mal would.

"Like this," Gen offered, and Mal joined in Levi's laughter but finally sat the way she should.

"I knew you'd be a good mom," Mal said as she sat back, her voice sounding almost hoarse. Or maybe that was her normal voice since Gen had never heard Mal speak.

Gen felt her heart swell in gratitude at Mal's words. She may not know the woman, but Gen had spoken to many, many women in her life and career, and she knew genuine when she heard it. Mal had been completely genuine.

"I'm Gen." Gen leaned across the couch to offer her hand.

"Mal," Mal responded as her light grip met Gen's.

"Thank you," Mal said as tears began to suddenly fall down her face. Mal looked from where Levi stood holding Maddie and back to Gen. "I know I don't deserve this. But Maddie does."

Gen finally gave in to the tears that had been threatening, and she quietly cried along with Mal.

Maddie wiggled out of her father's arms and her little legs went as fast as they could to her mother before she scrambled into Mal's lap and wiped the tears on her mother's face.

"Don't cry, Mama," Maddie said.

Mal laughed. "Isn't she perfect?"

Gen nodded. She absolutely was.

"I had hoped to see the three of you together. I have no idea what the other side holds for me. I hope God is as forgiving as you both have been. Maybe he can love his daughter beyond her mistakes. But getting to imagine Maddie's life after I'm gone, and not feeling completely terrified for once ... it's the biggest blessing. Thank you, Gen. Thank you for taking in my baby girl," Mal said as she hugged Maddie tight.

The tears fell harder down Gen's face as she watched Mal hug Maddie with a supernatural strength, considering how weak she was. This was what a mother's love was. And Gen hoped she could be enough for Maddie. Looking at Mal, she knew she could never replace the woman. She didn't want to. But she wanted Maddie to have a life where she had everything, including feeling like she had a mom.

"I'll do my best," Gen said.

Mal nodded. "I know you will."

Gen felt overwhelmed. But her work was done. She'd met Maddie and Mal, and she was completely enamored with the former as well as had no room for hate for the latter. She realized the gift Mal was bestowing on her. There was no way to hate a woman who had made this kind of sacrifice for her daughter.

"I should go," Gen said as she stood.

"Tomorrow is our last day here," Mal said and then kissed the top of Maddie's head. "I have to get back to my doctors. They weren't thrilled about this trip. But I told them if I was dying already, let me live the last days I have in the way I want to." Mal said the words lightly, but the implication behind them had Gen's chest constricting. Mal was dying, and she knew it.

"I don't think I have much longer. Maybe a few weeks, tops. Apparently my body chose to take on a fast moving cancer. They said I could go from walking and talking one day to completely comatose the next," Mal said.

Gen shook her head. She couldn't imagine.

"Would you two come as soon as you get the news? I don't want Maddie to feel a hole in her life, and I'm hoping you two will be the ones to fill the one I'm making," Mal said.

Gen could hardly believe her ears. Mal *wanted* to be replaced so that her daughter wouldn't hurt. That kind of pure love was beyond admirable.

"We'll be there," Gen promised, and she knew she would. She would have already moved mountains for Maddie, which was ridiculous since she'd barely met the girl. But she was also willing to do this for Mal. The woman who had slept with her husband. But after meeting Mal, it wasn't the way she saw her anymore. It was like that ghost of a woman had finally stopped haunting Gen. And the departure of that ghost gave her room to have compassion for the woman who sat in front of her.

"Thank you," Mal said as Maddie climbed down from her lap and went to a standing Gen.

Maddie put her arms up, and Gen immediately gave in to the invitation, snuggling the little girl close.

Maddie may not have come to Gen in the perfect way, but Gen knew in her heart that Maddie was the perfect child for her.

EIGHTEEN

IT WAS FINALLY the night before the food truck's grand opening, and Olivia felt akin to a zombie as she walked down Bess' driveway. She'd been at the food truck from dawn until dusk, and then at Bess' for the last four hours, finalizing every detail. But they were ready. Well as ready as they would ever be. Olivia was going to go down to the food truck with Bess at seven the next morning to get everything prepped before they opened for their first lunch service at eleven.

She blew out a sigh of relief. It felt good to be busy and have a purpose. Of course she'd always had a purpose as Rachel and Pearl's mother, but as they'd grown, she'd known she needed to add to her plate. This was just the right thing. Bess had been a Godsend, the kind of mentor that people only dreamed of, and getting to help Bess embark on one of the craziest adventures of her life was a blessing.

"Olivia?"

Olivia looked down the lamp-lit street to see the figure of a man and a dog. Thankfully she recognized that voice along with the dog or else she would have been intimidated. It was nearly midnight, and she was out on the street alone.

"You're out late," Dean said as he jogged up to her, and Olivia drank in the sight of the beautiful man. She'd seen teenager Dean without his shirt on, but this man before her was a far cry from the lanky kid he'd been. His broad shoulders rippled with muscle that ran down his lean, corded arms and, heaven help her, his abs were a sight to behold.

But he'd spoken to her. And she needed to respond. Ogling the man would help no one. Well, maybe Olivia a little. She'd enjoy her dreams a lot more if Dean were starring in them, but nope. She needed to get back to the conversation.

"I was over at Bess'. We needed to get the final details of the truck nailed down before tomorrow," Olivia said, trying her best to sound coherent as she pulled her eyes away from the abs and to the face of the man. Which she had to admit wasn't a downgrade in the least. Dean's body was an equal opportunity beauty zone.

The smirk on Dean's face when she met his eyes was easy to see, but she ignored his smug expression because what was she supposed to say? She probably could defend her actions and then ask him to wear a shirt, but she doubted that would result in anything less than a smirk as well.

"Right, that's tomorrow. I have it on my calendar that I'm getting lunch and dinner at Scratch Made by Bess."

"Thank you. We can use all the support we can get. This whole thing is so scary. I mean, we all know Bess' food is good. But what if ..."

"Tonight isn't the night for *what ifs*," Dean said. Then he was pulled a step closer to Olivia when his dog pulled on his leash to get closer to a bush he was inspecting.

The scent of sweat and salt air hit Olivia, and she knew she should be repulsed by the smell. But coming from Dean, it was manly and a little bit heady. She took a step back. She had no room for heady in her life.

"You're right. We're on this path, and ready or not, tomorrow will come," Olivia said, trying to focus on anything other than how good Dean looked and smelled.

"For what it's worth, I'm sure you guys will be a smashing success," Dean said with a grin.

Olivia smiled back. "For what it's worth, I'm grateful for your opinion," Olivia countered. Then she remembered the time. "But I'd better get to bed. Seven will be here before I know it."

Olivia turned to walk to her parents' house when Dean said, "I know things have been chaotic, for both of us. But ..." he paused as Olivia turned back to him, her face full of caution. "I'd love to have the girls come over and play with Buster when they have some time. I know he'd love it, and it seemed like they loved him."

Olivia nodded, immediately grateful that Dean hadn't asked her out. She was a little nervous the conversation had been heading in that direction, and she wasn't ready for Dean yet. She wanted to be, because he was the catch of a lifetime, but she wasn't there. And she didn't want to say no to a date with Dean because she was sure one day she'd want to say yes. It just wasn't that day yet.

"They've been bugging me about Buster at least once a week since that day at the park. We would all love that," Olivia said with a wide smile. But she really needed to go to bed since she was about to fall over on her feet.

"Good night, Dean," Olivia said as she turned and started toward home.

"Good night, Olivia," she heard him call after her.

Olivia grinned. She was pretty sure she was going to have an excellent dream starring Dean that night.

DEB SMILED as she looked at her latest painting. Gone were the blacks and reds; the purples, pinks, and blues of her soul were back. She had finally finished her Sunset on Whisling Island painting, and she knew exactly what she wanted to do with it.

"Mom, I'm going to Lexie's," Bailee said as she came to the doorway of Deb's art studio.

Things were still a little rough between mother and daughter, but they were working their way through things. Bailee had graduated from high school, and that transition without the divorce would have already been hard for Deb. Bailee was now officially an adult, and boy, did Bailee like to lord that over Deb's head. But she was also still under Deb's roof and would forever be her baby girl. There lay the rub, but Deb would figure it out.

Deb was also thrilled because Wes would be home in a week, spending almost the entire summer with his sister and Deb. Both of her children would be in London for a couple of weeks in the middle of the summer, terms of the finalized divorce agreement, but Deb would get them the rest of the time.

Rich had married his mistress as soon as the ink on their divorce papers was dry, and Deb had thought that idea would kill her. But she wasn't as upset as she thought she'd be. She was still sad about the loss of the future she'd imagined; however, her anger was gone. And boy was that freeing.

She and Rich were on civil terms. They'd never be best friends again, but they knew they had to keep some semblance of family for their kids' sakes. So they did their best to talk on the phone instead of texting every arrangement, and when Rich and his new wife had shown up to Bailee's graduation, Deb had had an entire conversation with Rich without a single argument. Considering she'd wanted to kill him not two months before, this was astounding progress.

"I think what you meant to say is, 'Mom, can I go to Lexie's?'" Deb said as she turned to her daughter.

"Mom, can I go to Lexie's?" Bailee asked.

"Sure. Just be home by midnight," Deb said. Then she fought off a smile as Bailee's face contorted.

"Mo-om," Bailee said.

"Fine, one," Deb said. Her daughter didn't seem happy, but then again, neither was Deb. One was too late but better than Bailee's idea that she not have a curfew.

"See you at one," Bailee groaned as she walked down the hall and then left the house.

Deb heard the door close behind her and was reminded, once again, that in just a few months, this house would be completely empty. Deb would be alone.

She shook her head free of the thoughts. Because she wasn't alone that night. And she had plenty to occupy her for the time being, considering she was in a rush to get to Bess' food truck before they closed for the evening.

Deb had been there for both lunch and dinner and had to wait in nearly an hour-long line each time. Those kinds of waits were unheard of on the island, and even though a few in line had seemed disgruntled about the wait, as soon as they got their food, no one seemed to mind. The grand opening had been a smashing success.

But Deb had wanted to get back to the truck by eight pm, right as Bess closed, to give her a gift.

Deb hurriedly wrapped the painting that she felt signified the past few months in both her and Bess' lives before getting in her car to make the drive into town.

NINETEEN

BESS FINALLY CLOSED the door of the food truck behind her for the last time that day. She'd have to be there again at eight am tomorrow—she and Olivia had streamlined things that morning so that they'd need an hour less of prep time the next day—but Bess was thrilled. She could spend all day every day on that truck. However, that didn't mean she wasn't exhausted by the end of the work day.

Clapping sounded as Bess turned to see Olivia, Gen, and Deb all sitting at one of the wooden tables with benches that Bess had had built for her customers. The seating options weren't plentiful but were just enough for the tourists who wanted to eat their meals there with the ocean view. Whereas most of the locals opted to take their food home.

Bess bowed. "Thank you," she said as she took a seat next to Deb and across from Olivia who sat next to Gen.

"But in all honesty, I should be clapping for you three. I couldn't have done it without you," Bess said.

Deb scoffed. "Maybe those two." Deb pointed to the two women who'd been in the truck all day with Bess. Bess would need to hire out some kitchen help soon, but she'd wanted to start with people she trusted, and Olivia and Gen had both obliged. Thankfully, the grand opening had been on Gen's day off, but she'd have to be back at the salon the next day. Bess would bet the number of their customers would go down the next day after all the hype had died off, but they could probably still use another hand or two in the kitchen, especially because this technically wasn't part of Olivia's job. "But I did nothing," Deb finished.

"You brought in hordes of customers," Bess said. She'd seen her friend hailing down cars that drove along Elliot Drive to bring them down to where Bess had parked her food truck.

"Hordes is an overstatement," Deb said.

Bess smiled. "And I wouldn't have survived the kitchen without you two," Bess said.

Olivia gave Bess a smile as Gen nodded. They knew it was the truth. The place had been a mad house. But they'd survived and maybe even thrived a little.

"I have something for you," Deb said as she pulled a paper wrapped gift from her lap onto the table in front of Bess.

Bess looked at her best friend, who just pumped her eyebrows sassily, before unwrapping the paper and then flipping over the framed painting.

"I thought you could hang it in the food truck," Deb said.

Bess felt her eyes fill with tears. She'd always known her best friend was talented, but this painting of a Whisling sunset was pristine. It not only captured the time of day with such precision it could have been a photograph, but the picture also captured the emotion of the time of day. The ending of light before a new day could begin.

"I'll do it proudly," Bess said, but she kept her eyes on her painting. She couldn't look away until she took in every detail.

"Deb, it's absolutely breathtaking," Gen said as Olivia added,

"Better than the real thing." Olivia pointed to the sky where the sun was just about to dip behind the horizon.

Waves lapped up onto the rocks below where they sat, about to soak up the last bits of light for the day. It was the perfect time of day to present this painting.

"I figure it's kind of a metaphor as well. We," Deb looked between herself and Bess and then at Gen and Olivia, "I guess all of us have experienced a sunset recently."

"And quite a bit of darkness," Gen added.

They sure had. Bess thought about how it had felt like her life was ending. She'd had a turbulent sunset, and in a way her life *had* ended. But although that sunset had given way to a long period of darkness, Bess could now start to see the faintest rays of a brand-new day in her future.

"But after sunset and the night, we get light again. It's bound to happen," Olivia said, and the other women nodded. Bess was sure they were all ready for their sunrises, and Bess had a feeling they'd be coming soon. But man, had they had to work for them.

"So, what do you call it?" Bess asked because she knew Deb gave each of her paintings a name.

"I kept it simple. Sunset on Whisling Island," Deb said.

Bess smiled. That was about as spot on as it could get. Bess would proudly display this painting of a day ending, and it would be a reminder to Bess that after every sunset came a sunrise.

CPSIA information can be obtained
at www.ICGtesting.com
Printed in the USA
LVHW011550290720
661860LV00013B/1060